TAPPING HER

A BILLIONAIRE

Bad Boys

NOVELLA

max monroe

Tapping Her: A Tapping the Bilionaire Novella
Published by Max Monroe LLC
© 2016, Max Monroe

ISBN-13: 978-1534691827
ISBN-10: 1534691820

Editing by Silently Correcting Your Grammar
Formatting by Champagne Formats
Cover Design by Perfect Pear Creative
Proofreading by Indie Solutions by Murphy Rae

DEDICATION

To the extra five pounds we gained while writing this novella: Fuck you.

And to donuts: You're delicious. Don't change.

CHAPTER 1

New York, Thursday, April 20ᵗʰ, Early Morning

Cassie

Georgia: Good Night from Bora Bora!

A h, Georgia. My beautiful, sweet, funny, newly married, currently annoying as *fuck* best friend.

Her lovely text included a photo of her and her hot husband, lounging in the tropical sun, on a private beach in Bora Bora. They'd been on their honeymoon for no more than three days, and I'd already received fifteen nauseatingly happy messages.

Me: You. Are. An. Asshole. Another picture of you and Big Dick at the beach, and I'll drop Walter off at the Humane Society.

Georgia: If you fuck with my cat, I will disown you.

Me: *Your cat is Satan. Seriously. I think the devil was reincarnated inside him. He's evil.*

Did I fail to mention that while Georgia and Kline were on their honeymoon, I had been given the responsibility of taking care of Walter? And not in the cool way that a mobster would. Georgie actually wanted me to look out for his *well-being*. Well, Thatch and I had been given that task, but I was the one at their apartment, spending time with their asshole of a cat.

Georgia might've thought he was a big sweetheart, but he was the opposite—a big feline dick. That cat's life mission was to make everyone else's life a living hell. And he did it often. So far, in the span of forty-eight hours, he'd pissed on my favorite pair of Chucks and left a generous gift of his shit—*yes, his actual cat shit*—inside my overnight bag.

Which explained why I was tits out, standing around in only my thong and rummaging through Georgia's closet. Fresh out of the shower, I needed something to wear that didn't smell like feline feces.

"Thanks a lot, douchenozzle," I said out loud, looking directly at Walter—who was currently lounging on their bed, licking himself. "Nice. Real classy, Walnuts."

He just stared back, irritated and completely aloof, all at once. I guess that's the look you get when a good fifteen hours of your day is used up by licking the rim of your own asshole. He eyed me for a solid ten seconds without a single blink and then strode out of the room, kitty paws tip-tapping across the hardwood floor. I couldn't put my finger on the exact reason, but everything about the way he moved screamed *fuck you.*

"Yeah, walk away, buddy! Walk the fuck away!" I shouted toward him as my phone vibrated on top of the dresser next to the closet.

Georgia: He is not evil! He's just a little hesitant with new people. He'll warm up to you.

Me: Ohhhhh…so when he pisses on my shoes, that's just him being "hesitant"? Or is that him "warming up to me"?

Georgia: Another 24 hours and you guys will be buddies. I promise.

Me: He shit inside my overnight bag, Wheorgie. This tells me that your promises mean nothing. I hope you don't mind me going through your closet. Because I already am.

Georgia: You can wear anything but my favorite LuLaRoe leggings.

Damn, she makes it too easy. Looks like hot dog leggings will be worn today.

For all I knew, those leggings were an inside joke about Kline packing a foot-long in his pants, but whatever. I'd make those stretchy pants my bitch. Hell, maybe I'd take a leisurely seventy-mile jog in Central Park just to make sure my twat left her mark.

Gross? Definitely.
But should I remind you her cat has been using my personal belong-ings as his litter box?
Point made.

Georgia: Wait. Why did you bring an overnight bag to my apartment?

Me: Because I'm watching The Asshole.

Georgia: That still doesn't answer my question. We just asked you to check in on Walter and feed him twice a day, not move in.

Me: Yeah, but I can't rummage through your kinky sex box at my apartment.

This was me calling Georgia's bluff. I had no idea if she had a freak-a-leek box of goodies, but I was real curious. She had always been a bit reserved when it came to sex. I mean, she was a virgin up until she let Big Dick inside. Which honestly surprised the shit out of me. It was how I knew, when she gave it up to Kline, he would become a permanent fixture in her life.

To quote Phoebe Buffay, *Kline Brooks was Georgia's motherfucking lobster.*

Okay, so the profanity was all mine. The lobster part was a la *Friends.*

Needless to say, I was the over-sharer in our relationship. Georgia had nailed down the "I don't kiss and tell" role from the very beginning. And I couldn't deny the enjoyment I got from pushing her boundaries and making her blush.

Georgia: Do NOT go through my shit, Casshead.

Me: But this vibrator looks really cool. And a ball gag? Shit, G, I didn't know you had it in you. Color me impressed. Kline's dick looks good on you.

Georgia: Shut. Up. I'm done with this conversation.

Holy mother of awesome. My best friend had a stash full of sex goodies somewhere in her apartment, and I was going to find it.

Me: I was kidding. But now, I'm not kidding. Canceling my "get rid of Walnuts" mission. New mission: Find Georgia's box of freak. I'm so proud of you.

Georgia: Greetings from Bora Bora, asshole!

Attached to that text? A lovely picture of Georgia flipping me off while she stood on a deserted beach, twinkling water and her fucking beaming, handsome husband behind her.

Me: One question before I start my search in your closet. Do you clean your bag o' dildos after each use? Because if you don't, you'll need to pick up a new box of magnums on the ride home. I don't have any latex gloves, and one of these isn't big enough for my whole hand.

Georgia: You've already gone through Kline's nightstand?!

Me: Oh, come on. That's the first place you ALWAYS look. Does Kline really fill the entire magnum? Because if he does, I'm convinced his cock is a mythical unicorn.

Georgia: I'm not discussing my husband's penis with you.

Me: Haha! I could literally hear you say the word penis like a schoolmarm. "Peeee-nis."

Georgia: I'm disowning you when I get back from my honeymoon.

Me: Just remember to pick up milk too on your way home. You're almost out.

Georgia: Since you've made yourself at home. House rules: NO sex in my bed.

Me: Okay, but those rules start right now, right? Yesterday shouldn't count.

Don't worry, I'm not that much of a weirdo. I don't make a point of using my best friend's bed as my own personal brothel. But it's too funny not *to make her think that.*

Georgia: WASH MY SHEETS.

Me: I love you, Wheorgie. Go back to enjoying your honeymoon and riding Kline's peee-nis with the glow of the sunset behind you. I'll take care of everything here like it's my own.

Georgia: Ugh. I love you too, Casshead. Replace everything you destroy.

I swear, my best friend was far too easy to rile up. I probably shouldn't get that much amusement out of it, but I did. She pulled off adorably embarrassed like no one else. And I wasn't the only one who noticed. Kline used it to his advantage, *frequently*. It was one of the reasons I loved him. He knew Georgia better than she knew herself sometimes, and he also respected her, cherished her, and treated her like a goddamn princess—all the requirements for avoiding genital mutilation, courtesy of me.

Since I was alone and there was absolutely nothing more fun than walking around without a bra on, I stopped my clothes search and placed my phone in their speaker dock. Once my playlist was set, it was time to search this place like I was a key investigator for the FBI.

Rhianna's "Cockiness" was speaking to me, echoing throughout the apartment and getting my exploration mojo off to the right start.

"I love it when you eat it," I sang, shaking my hips to the seductive beat and moving back toward Georgie's closet.

And then, in my peripheral vision, my eyes caught sight of a large, looming figure in the doorway.

"Ahhhhh!" I screamed. "Holy son of a whore tramp!"

CHAPTER 2

Thatch

Fucking fuck.

I mean, fuck me.

No.

Titty-fuck me.

"Helloooo?" Cassie's perfect, heavy tits said while they swung back and forth, free from cover and uninhibited by clothing or bra. "Hey, fuckface!" they yelled. "Are you perverted or just dumb? The normal amount of time to stare at someone uninvited passed like forty-five seconds ago."

God, not only were they the perfect size and shape, they were fucking smart. Speaking in full sentences and shit. This had to be the most talented pair of tits I'd ever encountered. They sounded a little agitated, but I was pretty sure that was just a side effect of the blood roaring in my ears.

"Ow!" I flinched as Cassie grabbed my nipple through the fabric of my dress shirt and twisted. "Jesus! What the fuck?"

"What the fuck? I'll tell you what the fuck. You've been staring at my chest for the last two minutes!"

I watched as her mouth moved, even heard it form the words, but try as I might, I couldn't *not* notice that *they* still hung there, uncovered in all their perfect, creamy, pink-tipped glory. When they swung toward me again with her lunge, I forced my eyes back to her wildly beautiful face.

"Look, I'm sorry. But they're out and they're perfect and they were fucking *talking* to me."

I pressed a hand to the uncontrollably swelling cock in my pants. She raised an eyebrow in response.

On my way to work, I'd decided I should do my bit for the cat, see if I needed to order an exorcist, that kind of thing, but I wasn't expecting tits. And my cock certainly wasn't expecting them to be so perfect. But, first thing in the morning like this, it was no wonder I couldn't control his desire to crow.

"My tits don't talk." She turned her back, and I trained my eyes hard enough that they almost bore their way through to the other side. Voice muffled a little by the still-playing music, she went on. "They bounce and swing and wrap just about perfectly around a worthy cock, but they don't speak."

"I don't believe you," I argued. "They spoke to me, and I'll take that reality to the grave."

"You're fucked in the head, you know that?" she asked as she sauntered brazenly across the room to Kline's closet and pulled it open. The light went on, illuminating the space, and she bent over, her bare ass up and out, and started rummaging around.

"What are you doing?" I asked, giving the base of my cock a healthy squeeze in an attempt to choke the overzealous life out of it.

"Looking for Georgie and Big Dick's box of kink," was the mumbled reply.

I turned away and crossed the room, eager to find some kind of solace.

"Oh. It's under the bed," I said as I closed my eyes tight and flopped back onto it. Hard and hurting, my dick had taken over, and there was absolutely no hope of a resolution until I stopped looking at all of her flawless skin.

"Oh, shit," she squealed. The sound of her running toward me gave me a mental image of her body in motion that would likely be the largest test of willpower my eyes ever had or would receive. I stayed frozen, hand locked on my easily manipulated dick and eyes sealed completely.

"How the hell did you find this before I did?" she complained from below me, the bed shaking slightly from her effort to pull out the box of phallic treasure.

"I found that shit months ago, about two days after they moved in together."

She pulled the box out, dumping it on the bed right beside my head and tossing her body below it, right next to my hip. At the feel of some piece of her skin brushing against my hand, my eyes gave up the fight and popped open faster than a jack-in-the-box.

"Good God," I cried when my vision returned. She was on her hands and knees, digging through the pile of dicks and vibrators beside my head, and her naked tits were no more than ten inches from my lips. "Am I dead?" I whispered, staring at the pink of her nipples and licking my lips.

Is this heaven or hell?

My hand wouldn't be denied, reaching out to test my location. When the soft, full, *fucking perfect* flesh of her breast met my greedy palm, she yelped, smacking me first on the hand and then on the face.

"Ouch!" I groaned before confirming, "Hell."

Definitely hell.

"What?" she snapped. "You can look, but you'll have to do a lot more to earn the right to touch."

My lips pursed in thought. "I could—"

"Not today, asshat!" she yelled. "Come on, help me clean this shit up."

In shock, I couldn't do anything other than what she asked, touching my best friend's things—things I swear I'd never otherwise touch—and completely abandoning thoughts of being on time for work or accomplishing anything I was supposed to that day.

And yes, I'm sure I wouldn't normally touch them. Look, sure. Touch, no.

Cassie left me to finish up and crossed the room back to Georgie's dresser, my gaze following her as she did. She was one of the hottest women I'd ever seen and the first ever to stand in front of me naked with the same confidence as she would if clothed. I didn't know where she found that kind of self-esteem, and I wasn't going to ask. The first rule of dealing with a woman without her clothes on is to never ask her anything that could lead to a change of heart.

I slid the box under the bed as she slipped a tight T-shirt over her head, sans bra, and stepped into a pair of what had to be the most ridiculous leggings I'd ever seen.

"Are there fucking hot dogs on those pants?"

"Yeah," she deadpanned, turning to face me and pulling her crazy hair into a sloppy ponytail. As her nipples pushed through the thin cotton, I realized no one would give a goddamn what was on her bottom half.

She turned for the hall, stepping out of the room without a word, and I followed. I'd have followed her into a volcano at this point.

And yes, I am fully aware that this kind of blind arousal will be my downfall.

"Hey, Walnuts!" she called when we made it to the living room, searching the space with her strikingly blue eyes. They were so vivid they were nearly violent, reaching out and smacking you every time they turned your way.

The contrast between them, her creamy white skin, and the rich chocolate of her hair was arresting. Like God had a sense of humor when he made her, pasting together all the things that shouldn't go well together into a singular messy canvas, but when he was done— her magnificently wild radiance shone *up* to heaven. The joke was on him.

"Yo! Walnuts!" she called again. "I'm talking to you, dick cat! Food's on!"

She turned to me with her eyebrows pinched together, and the simple gesture was enough to break me out of my stupor.

I joined in the search, scanning the room endlessly, and unfortunately, my eyes landed on the open apartment door at the same time Cassie's did.

Shit.

"You idiot!" she yelled, charging for the door and tearing ass out into the hall.

I followed hot on her heels, pulling her to a stop before she got to the stairwell door and spinning her to face me.

When I'd come in and heard the music, I hadn't thought of anything but finding the source. I wasn't used to having a pet, so closing doors wasn't naturally ingrained. It probably would be now.

"You lost Walter!" she screamed immediately.

"You don't know that," I argued. "He could still be in the apartment somewhere."

"He's not! That little ass-licker does a lot of stupid things, but he doesn't skimp on meal times. If you'd helped me feed him at all, you would know that!"

"Cass, calm down."

"I will not calm down!" she screeched.

I reached out to lay a reassuring hand on her arm at the same time another tenant stepped out of the adjacent apartment.

Prim and proper, the conservative woman wrinkled her nose at Cassie's outfit and pinched her eyes at me. "All this yelling. I thought this apartment building had a better handle on class."

Cass turned in a flourish, cocking her head to the side and getting right in the offender's face. "I will go Holly Holm on your ass!"

I jumped into action, wrapping my arms around her and copping a small feel in the process. She burned me with her eyes, and I tried not to smile, but as I turned back to the *still open* apartment door, Walter scurried out like a shot and turned the corner in a flash. Releasing Cass, I traveled the space in as few steps as my giant legs would allow, but when I rounded the bend, not a whisker or a hair remained.

Ah, *fuck*.

The dick cat hadn't been missing, but he sure as fuck was now.

CHAPTER 3

Bora Bora, Thursday, April 20th, Morning

Georgia

Glancing at the clock on the bedside table, I could see 7:00 a.m. glowed red and bright. My internal clock was still on East Coast time, and I had started a bad habit of napping in the midafternoon sun for the past three days. Sounds of the ocean filtered through the open terrace doors, a warm breeze brushing across the room and filling it with aromas of salt water and sand.

Stupidly happy. Thoroughly well-fucked. Blissfully sated.

No doubt, I was all of those things.

The sole reason lay beside me, sprawled out on his back, with soft, white sheets barely covering his deliciously naked form. Kline was sound asleep, hair mussed up and a small grin etched across his full lips. He had passed out that way after round three—*or was it four?*—and that little expression of appreciation had stayed intact for the past hour. Since round four had been an oral experiment in showing him just how much I loved him, I'd say his sexy grin was a direct result of my mouth.

We had been on our honeymoon for three days, and I still needed to pinch myself to believe it was real. That he—my handsome, charming, undeniably romantic *husband*—was real. We still had another week and a half to enjoy our privacy in Bora Bora, but I was already feeling grumpy over the idea of returning home and leaving our little slice of tropical heaven.

I grabbed my phone from the nightstand and scrolled through numerous emails. One from my boss, Kline's good friend Wes, urged a quick response.

To: Georgia.Brooks@Mavericks.com
From: Wes.Lancaster@Mavericks.com

Georgia,

I hope you and Kline are enjoying your honeymoon. If you can spare a few minutes away from your husband, I'd be forever in your debt if you could take a glance at this contract. If he gives you grief, just send him my way. I'd really like your opinion on this offer before we pull the trigger.
Wes Lancaster
President and Chief Executive Officer
New York Mavericks
National Football League

The contract in question was for a sports drink campaign. I couldn't deny the drink tasted like gasoline, but the VITAsteel brand had been growing in popularity over the past three years and had made quite the name for itself in the sports industry. Professional athletes across the globe fell over themselves to land an endorsement with this company. And even though the Mavericks were knocked out in the first-round playoffs last year, I had managed to get some raised eyebrows of intrigue over at VITAsteel when I proposed a contract that included our quarterback *and* offensive line.

See? I was starting to understand football lingo. Of course, I still nicknamed all of our players, but no one needed to know that.

I read through the contract and sent a quick email back to Wes, highlighting the things I didn't like. The offer was good, but it could be better. First rule of business, always be prepared to negotiate and *never* take the first offer that's sent your way. My business-savvy husband taught me that.

Considering I was getting emails from my boss during my honeymoon, I'd say it was obvious work was about to get a bit intense for me. The New York Mavericks were in the midst of a marketing overhaul and rebranding, and since I was leading this insane task, my job would require more than a simple, forty-hours-a-week schedule. Late nights, gallons of coffee, and a shitload of frequent flyer miles were about to fill my future.

I had a feeling Kline wasn't going to swallow this pill all that well.

My husband was understanding to a fault, but he had gotten used to me being by his side at the office for the early part of our relationship, and even after I had taken the job with the Mavericks and we had managed to find our way back to one another, my work hours were manageable. He'd been making a real effort to leave work at five o'clock, and I'd done the same. But my workload was about to increase tenfold. Who wants to hear that kind of news from their brand-new wife?

And if I was being honest, I wasn't all that thrilled with the idea of less time with him either. I hated it, actually. But my career was important to me. The drive to pave out my own kind of success ran deep. I wanted, no, *needed,* to accomplish the goals I had set for myself.

Finding the right balance and some serious understanding on

my husband's part was going to be key in making it all work without one of us going crazy. We had talked about my soon-to-be demanding schedule and traveling with the team for away games, but with the craziness of the wedding, we never really had a chance to sit down and map it all out.

That conversation would come, but right now, in this perfect little moment, other things would have to *come* first. Big-dicked kind of things.

Before I got down and dirty with Kline, I glanced at the clock again, and knowing that it was six hours later in New York, I sent Cass a quick text message.

Me: How's Walter?

Cassie: He's great! Eating, shitting, pissing, and just doing his normal cat thing around your apartment.

My eyebrows rose at that response. I had expected something more like, "*He's a fucking asshole, but still alive.*" Maybe he had finally warmed up to Cass?

Cassie: And I gotta say, the amount of kinky sex shit you've got stored under your bed is INSANE. My Wheorgie is definitely letting her freak flag fly.

Ugh. I debated telling her the truth about the giant box of kink under our bed. They were all generous and, no doubt, weird gifts from my mother. Since we got engaged, Kline and I had been receiving brand-new toys on the regular from Dr. Savannah Cummings. My crazy mother was convinced we needed to explore our sexuality together, in *every* possible way. Anal beads, ball gags, twelve-inch dildos, you name it, and it was shipped to our apartment.

Thatch found the box while helping us move in, and I swear to God, he wouldn't shut up about it. Hell, he still sent me random text messages asking if I wear Ben Wa balls to work.

The thing my mother didn't understand was that I didn't need thousands of kinky toys when I had Kline. A vibrator was no match for his PhD in Sexual Prowess. I'd actually suggested he teach a course at NYU one night after sex. He'd laughed, but I was serious. The female population of Manhattan *needed* him. I brought it up every so often, but he wasn't going for it. He said he was in charge of keeping exactly one pussy happy, and that position was all filled.

And, yes, I agree. I'm one lucky bitch. Don't worry, I remind myself of this fact at least one hundred times a day.

Kline stirred a little in his sleep, one arm reaching out across the bed and stopping once it met the skin of my hip. For a moment, I just soaked up the sight of him. Hair in disarray and a few days' worth of scruff peppering his jaw, my husband was so goddamn sexy I could hardly stand it. Over the past few days, we'd been doing nothing but climbing inside one another. The sex had been intense, crazy, and incredibly hedonistic. And I would ensure it continued that way for the duration of our honeymoon.

I set my phone down on the nightstand and decided it was time to give my husband a wake-up call. Remembering a conversation Kline and I had yesterday while we were lying under the sun, I decided to return the favor of him giving me a little striptease the night we skinny-dipped at ONE UN.

Gently, so I wouldn't wake him, I slid out from under his arm and crossed the length the spacious bedroom in our bungalow. I put on the only pair of black heels I had brought with me and wrapped my short, silk robe around my body, tying it loosely at my waist.

Once Zayn's "Pillowtalk" was playing from the speakers of the

Bose sound system in the bedroom, I turned it *way* up, the beat of the seductive music overpowering the ocean waves.

Facing the bed, I waited for my husband to stir from his precious beauty sleep. His eyelids fluttered, sleepy blue gaze meeting mine, and he rubbed at his face, slowly sitting up and resting against the headboard. The sheet fell away from his hips, revealing an already impressive erection, but he wasn't all the way there, *not yet,* though he would be soon.

"Baby?" he asked, slightly disoriented yet getting harder with each scan his gaze took of my body.

"Good morning," I said, slowly moving my hips to the music.

He tilted his head to the side, eyeing me with equal parts amusement and desire.

"Don't mind me," I teased, turning my back to him and untying my robe. The silk material slid down a bit, revealing the skin of my shoulders. I glanced back at him, winking. "I just felt like dancing a little. You can go back to sleep if you want."

He chuckled, shaking his head. "No, thanks. I think I'll stay awake for this." He fluffed some pillows behind his head and sat up a little, cocking a knee so his erection stood out. "Yeah, I'll just lie here and enjoy my wife taunting me with her luscious ass."

"You want me to keep dancing?" I asked, turning around and holding my robe closed, but still moving to the lust-fueled beat of the music.

"Fuck yeah. Keep doing that." Kline nodded, slowly stroking himself as he watched me. "But lose the robe, Benny."

God, he was hot. It took all of my willpower to continue dancing and not climb on top of him.

"Patience, husband." I shook my head and waggled my index finger at him.

He grinned and scooted forward to sit on the edge of the bed, crooking his finger at me in a "come-hither" motion. "Get that gorgeous body over here."

"You got plans for me, baby?" I asked, raising an eyebrow.

"Oh, sweet Benny. You know you know the answer to that."

The heat in his eyes had a full-body blush overwhelming my skin. I couldn't help it; this man still had the power to turn me on with one sexy glance.

I made my way toward the bed, my movements still mimicking the music. Once I was in front of him, I rested my heel-clad foot on the mattress, beside his knee. The robe glided away from my hips and revealed me bared and wet for him. Only him. *Always* him.

"Fuck, baby." His eyes consumed me. Hands to my hips, he pulled me closer, head leaning toward my waist and devious tongue sneaking out to lick along my inner thighs.

My hips jerked toward him, unable to maintain any sort of rhythm. His mouth on me would always be my undoing.

Kline's hands pushed the robe off my shoulders, the material sliding down my body and falling to the floor in a puddle of silk. His mouth pressed against my pussy and he moaned, his lips vibrating against my wanton skin. "This," he whispered, tongue flicking against my clit. "This is exactly how I want to wake up every fucking morning for the rest of my goddamn life."

My head fell back, and a whimper spilled from my throat as he pushed a finger inside of me.

"Fuck, you're so wet."

"Yes," I moaned, my hips moving with the rhythm of his mouth and hand.

"I think I'll eat this perfect, delicious pussy for breakfast, and then feed you my cock when I'm done. Does that sound good, baby?"

"God, yes."

Within seconds, I was on the bed, lying flat on my back with my legs hanging over his shoulders as Kline made good on his promise.

And boy, oh boy, did he make good on it. The Kline and Georgie honeymoon bubble was officially my favorite place on earth.

CHAPTER 4

Kline

"Benny?" I called as I ran a hand through my damp, fresh-from-a-shower hair and padded across the bungalow's light wood floors.

She didn't answer immediately, but fuck, I wouldn't have either. The place was two stories, ostentatious, and bigger than our Manhattan apartment, so hearing each other wasn't exactly easy. When the hotel had heard my name and that it was our honeymoon, they'd insisted on *making it special*. I was all for that. Georgie deserved the best, and it wasn't like I couldn't afford to give it to her. But I'd honestly thought they'd realize I'd actually want to *see* my bride on our honeymoon. It felt like I spent two hours out of every day just hunting her down.

"Georgie?" I yelled as I came down the staircase to the first floor. I knew I wouldn't find her in the ocean on her own, but the private pool was completely fair game.

We'd had a morning of nothing but fucking and flirting, and I couldn't wait to spend the rest of the day the same way. I'd tried to convince her to shower the stickiness of our lovemaking off with me, but she'd conned me out of it with a flutter of her eyes and a pout of her lips.

That woman fucking owned me.

At the bottom of the steps, I looked from one end of the airy space to the other and then stepped out onto the back deck to look over the pool.

Nothing.

When I turned to head back into the overwater monstrosity, there she sat, her lounge chair tucked into the shady corner with her laptop in her sun-kissed lap.

Busy and buried in a menial task she shouldn't have been doing on our honeymoon, she hadn't even noticed I was there.

"Baby," I greeted softly, stepping under the shade of the porch and directly into her line of sight. Her eyes moved slowly, practically crawling their way off the page, but when they finally landed on me, they nearly bugged all the way out of her head.

"Kline!"

"Yeah, baby," I said with a smile. "That's me."

"And that's your—"

"Big-dicked Brooks. Right again, sweetheart."

"But we're outside! What if someone sees you?" she insisted, looking frantically back and forth around our empty patio and then back to me.

"You mean out in the middle of the ocean?" I asked, turning to point to the only aspect of our bungalow that I truly appreciated— privacy. At the end of a long line of over water huts, the back of our getaway faced no one. So few humans, so much creation. It was our own tropical paradise at the end of the world.

"Well, what if someone comes by in a kayak?"

I waggled my eyebrows and sauntered up close, looking her right in the eyes. "If you're really worried about someone seeing it, I know *just* the place to hide it."

"*Kline.*"

"Yeah. You'll definitely say my name."

"I just have to finish answering this email," she declared, but her eyes strayed to my cock more than one time and lingered on the second. When she rubbed her legs together, I couldn't resist.

One inch, two, I slid my hand up the silky smooth skin of her shin and her knee, and then turned to torture the meat at the inside of her thigh. It was slick with a mix of apple lotion and sweat, and every glossy knead made me want to eat up another sweet spot.

Her eyes glazed over, lost in me and the moment, and it was all I could do to put my free hand to use anywhere other than inside her tiny bikini. But I did, shutting her laptop with a snap and yanking it away just as she came out of her arousal-induced trance.

"I needed to finish that!"

"You need to come play with me," I countered, and her eyes narrowed as I did. I leaned in slowly and licked the line of her jaw before nibbling at the lobe of her ear with my teeth.

She smiled, looking out at the ocean and realizing where we were and exactly what I meant. "Okay. Let's play," she agreed seductively.

I bit my lip just as she reached out and took hold of my hard and waiting dick, and the flimsy string at her hips gave way easily, untying with one simple yank. Flipping her around and letting the scrap of white fabric drop to the deck, I settled my back into the chair and brought her down on me in one full stroke.

"Mmm," she moaned. Her head dropped back, and she shoved her tits closer to my mouth.

God, I loved when she did that. It was one of my favorite things, one of many in a collection of tiny, involuntary indications that she loved me, wanted me—needed me—as much as I did her.

"Do they ache, baby?" I whispered, reaching around behind her to untie the strings of her triangle top.

"Mmhmm, God, yes," she managed, nodding her head and pulling her hair up off her shoulders and into a messy pile on her head. Her cheeks were flushed, and a few flecks of salty moisture from the air dotted the tips of her long eyelashes.

I grabbed her other cheeks and spread them as I lifted. She gasped, and before she could finish, I slammed her back down until I was seated fully inside. Her pussy spasmed around me. "Yeah, Benny. Just like that. Milk my cock until I come, okay?"

"*Kline*. Please."

She never took long like this, when I caught her by surprise and demanded agreement from her body. My Georgie loved the way I took control—gently teasing her with flattering demands and arousing compliments. But it had been a while since she'd ignited *this* quickly.

"Are you already close, baby?"

One heady moan.

I had a feeling my shy little Benny was enjoying the idea of someone seeing a lot of things they shouldn't.

"Need me to suck on these perfect tits?" I asked, pulling the dangling fabric over her head and tossing it to the side. Her nipples pebbled, and a shiver ran through her body. I closed one in the heat of my mouth and sucked until she started to ride me on her own. Uninhibited. Desperate. She'd passed the point of waiting for me to give her what she needed.

Oh, yeah.

"That's it, baby. Take us both there," I whispered into the skin of her chest. She tightened around me and cried out, throwing her head back until the ends of her hair tickled the sensitive skin of my thighs and pushed me right over the edge with her.

Our breaths came out in a ragged rhythm, one following the other, until the air around us filled the capacity of our lungs.

I kissed the skin of her neck and sucked a sweet spot into the hollow at the center while she breathed out every ounce of hoarded air at once.

"You ready to play now, Benny?"

"Huh?" She laughed, blue eyes blazing through her backlit shadow. "Play now? I thought that was the play."

"Uh-uh," I denied. "*That* was me *making love* to my *wife.*"

A smile belied the shake of her head as she leaned forward and sealed her rosy lips to mine. "I love you," she said before rubbing her nose along the line of mine.

"I know," I whispered. "Now come gallivant in the ocean with me."

Her nose scrunched up in denial. "You had me until *in the ocean.*"

I picked her up and set her on her feet before climbing to my own. "Put your bikini back on and wait for me right here. I'm going to grab some trunks, and I don't want to fucking lose you again," I instructed, completely ignoring her aversion to all things sea life. She'd come around once we were in.

"Goddammit," she grumbled under her breath, scooping up the bottom of her bathing suit as she did.

"Don't worry, Benny. It's gonna be fun."

"Yeah, yeah," she agreed, tying the sides closed.

One gentle kiss to the corner of her lips and I pulled her to my chest. "Stay here. I'll be right back."

"Oh, no worries there. I won't be in the ocean without you, that's for sure."

I gave her another kiss and chuckled as I turned to run up the stairs and grab a swimsuit. When I came back, she was standing in the same spot, unfortunately un-naked, and the red-painted toes of her bare foot tapped nervously on the wood planks of the deck.

"Let's go," I said, spinning her around and pushing her forward with a gentle but insistent hand on her back. She paused at the edge, scanning the water for lurking creatures of terror.

"I'll go in first," I offered, stepping to the side and making my way down the ladder next to her. "See?" I asked, when water submerged the lower half of my body. "Nothing to worry about."

Her eyes narrowed, but she moved to the ladder, making her way down it tentatively and tapping a toe on the sandy bottom.

"Baby," I said through a laugh. "You can see the bottom. The water is crystal clear. What are you worried about?"

"It doesn't matter that the water is clear! This is a game of volume, Kline, and there's a fucking lot of water here. Something could sneak up on me."

"I won't let it," I pledged, crossing an *X* over my heart to seal the promise. She shook her head and worried her lip, but I pulled her off the ladder and into my arms anyway.

She wrapped her legs around my waist easily, and my hands found a comfortable home on her ass. I'd take frightened Georgia any day of the week if it meant she held on this tight.

When I started to rub at the soft flesh, she caught wind of my enjoyment. It probably had something to do with my inability to stop fucking smiling.

"You like that I'm scared, don't you?"

"I wouldn't say I *like* it…" I said in an attempt to avoid ruining my perfectly crafted plan.

Her eyes narrowed, and a hand slapped at the skin of my back. "You're right. You don't like it. You *love* it!" she accused.

"Okay, yeah," I agreed with a telling smirk. "Your body is basically fused to mine, and your ass is in my hands. Of course, I love it."

Her lips met mine actively, aggression and acceptance all at once. My mouth fought back until it won dominance, taking so much that it started to give.

Foreheads together, we stood there, the sound of our breathing and each other the only thing to keep us company in the emptiness of endless ocean.

Or so I thought.

Behind her back, I saw it approach, but I kept a careful watch on the state of my body in order to keep her unaware. A lone stingray swooped and swept its way along the bottom, cruising beautifully straight for us. I watched, glancing at Georgia briefly and waiting for her to notice.

Stepping to the side as the friendly ray drew near, I craned my neck as he circled behind us.

"Oh, sweet fucking Jesus!" Georgie shouted as soon as she saw it, climbing even higher up my body with the agility of a monkey. "Oh, my God!" she yelled. "Kline! Oh, Jesus!"

I started to laugh, but my Benny wasn't laughing at all.

"Help! Help us!"

Shit.

"Georgie, calm down," I cooed softly in an attempt to soothe her. But yeah, I also laughed again, and I knew that didn't help. Limbs flailed, and her eyes grew to twice their original size.

"You calm down, you fucking honeymoon murderer! This is all a ploy, right? I've seen those movies on Lifetime!"

"Oh, my God," I said through my laughter. "Baby, it's just a stingray."

"A fucking death ray!" she screeched from atop my shoulders. I wasn't even sure how she'd gotten there, but I *was* pretty sure it would end in a black eye. My face already throbbed. "You don't use your money for much, but that's because you saved it all up for an untraceable way to kill me, didn't you?"

"Ben—"

"Oh, my God! *Help us!* Call the fucking Coast Guard!"

We were in the middle of nowhere, but not *that* in the middle of nowhere. Fuck. Officials and hotel staff would be descending on us in no time.

"Georgie—"

"Shit! Oh, shit, Kline! He's circling. This is what they do before they strike!" she screamed, and I was reasonably certain my eardrums were bleeding.

"Baby," I said through a grimace. "It's a stingray, not a shark."

Sure, stingrays weren't completely benign, but I'd read all about their frequent tendency to swim among tourists without incident before I'd booked our honeymoon. As long as we were watchful, I didn't see the harm.

"THERE. ARE. SHARKS?!"

So much for calming her down…

"Your plan is fucked! He's going to kill us both!" Her hands were in my hair by that point, yanking the strands with a strength I had no idea she possessed. "Get me the fuck out of here before I end you!"

Unwilling to torture her until both of my eyes were bloodied, I laughed and waded my way to the ladder. I'd thought being close to safety would bring her some comfort, that the idea of an escape route would be enough, but she jumped from my shoulders to the deck without even touching a rung before I could stop her.

"That's it!" she said, pointing at me. "That's the last time I go in the water."

"We're in an over-water bungalow for another week and a half! What do you mean that's the last time?"

"Nope. Nuh-uh. Not gonna happen. If you want me dead, you're just going to have to figure out another way."

CHAPTER 5

Georgia

I pressed my hand against my chest, and my heart pounded against my fingertips, wild and erratic, all thanks to my husband who was still in the water, watching me have a minor—*okay, huge*—freak-out on the deck above him. His eyes were amused, mouth set in a tickled grin.

His crystal-blue gaze turned heated in a flash as it made a circuit of my dripping wet, bikini-clad body.

If I hadn't almost *died,* I might've been turned on.

But I *had* been mere moments from sleeping with the fishes rather than swimming with them, and my otherwise sweet husband found it nothing but comical.

No matter how brutally I stared at him, his smirk never diminished, playful eyes branding me as his and threatening to hump me in broad daylight.

"Don't smolder at me!" I shouted down to him, my feet still firmly planted on our deck.

No way in hell would I ever let him coax me into the sea of death again.

I enjoyed the view of the ocean, but savoring it from the sand or the pool was as far as I preferred to go. Sea creatures of all kinds creeped me the fuck out. Small ones flitted and flaunted, nibbling at your legs when you least expected it, and anything bigger could swallow you whole. No fucking thanks. No man, orgasm expert or not, was going to talk me into seeing it a different way.

"I'm not smoldering, baby." He held up both hands, an irritating display of the exact opposite of innocent. "I'm just enjoying the view that is my beautiful, riled up wife."

How could he smile when I had just been three seconds away from seeing the light?

With annoyance, I watched Kline run a hand through his hair. Droplets of water slipped from those wet locks down his chest, until they disappeared south of his belly and back into the ocean.

Okay, so I wasn't *that* annoyed. But I was doing my best to keep up appearances.

"I'm going inside to make some lunch." I grabbed a towel off one of the lounge chairs on the deck. "*You* can stay out here and risk your life, but *I'm* not going to be a part of it," I huffed over my shoulder as I strode toward the interior of our bungalow. Well, I should say, *sashayed*, because yeah, my ass was a superpower when it came to my husband.

"Bring that sexy ass back here."

"Not a chance!"

"But I love you, Benny! You and your ass. I *really* love your ass."

"Trying to off me is an odd way of showing it!"

"*Baby*, don't be mad," he called from behind me in that tone he knew usually worked like a charm. It was annoyingly sweet yet husky in a way that only Kline could pull off.

Not gonna work this time, buddy.

I flipped him off over my shoulder, and his chuckles followed me inside.

"Save me some food!"

I turned around and peeked out the deck doors. His back was to me as he stretched his arms for a swim. The muscles in his arms, legs, hell, *everywhere*, were as defined as ever. God bless his aptitude for keeping his body in tip-top shape.

He wasn't the kind of guy who "worked out" at the gym. He liked to *do* things to keep his physique, whether it was rugby or running or fucking his wife into a goddamn coma. His energy was endless, and he'd already spent hours on our honeymoon swimming laps in the pool while I slept myself back to fighting form in the sun. If my ass was my superpower in our relationship, my husband's stamina was its match.

Well, that and his cock. Because, yeah…*Big-dicked Brooks.*

"If I make you lunch, I need at least an hour of you *eating dessert* in return," I demanded while continuing to take in the sight of his ogle-worthy body.

He turned toward my voice, and his mouth curled up at the corners. "Promise?"

I shrugged. "I guess we'll have to see how persuasive that mouth of yours is."

"Mmm, I can't wait. I think I'll just live off your pussy for the rest of our honeymoon."

That comment had me smiling and blushing at once.

"Draft the contract, Brooks. I'll be back in a few," he said with a wink, rapping on the wood of the deck with his knuckles.

I watched as he turned and dove into the sea. His arms sliced through the calm waters in precise movements as he headed for the horizon. Man, he was almost as good at swimming as he was at fucking my brains out. And let's face it, Kline Brooks could *work* it.

I stood there for a good five minutes, stupid smile still intact, until my growling stomach forced my focus to food. Heading into the kitchen, I turned on my laptop and set the mood with a little Bob

Marley on my Spotify. And then I got to work, rummaging through the stocked fridge for ingredients. In the mood for something light and savory, I began making a chicken Caesar salad. Sure, we could have had room service delivered on a regular basis, but both me and Kline preferred to keep our honeymoon mostly to ourselves without the threat of even tiny interruptions.

Once the food was ready, and I had changed into a yellow cotton sundress, I stood at the breakfast bar and dug into the crisp salad while going through some emails.

The only one that needed an urgent reply was another one from Wes. I was starting to wonder if he was doing this on purpose, attempting to distract me, his best friend's wife, while on my honeymoon. It wouldn't surprise me if that was his game. The trio, aptly nicknamed Billionaire Bad Boys, tended to give each other shit as often as possible. It was a wonder they had time to do anything else. At least everyone else seemed to be getting the *Leave Georgia Alone* memo.

I promptly read through the newly drafted contract for VITAsteel. It looked a hell of a lot better than the original proposed deal, but I still wasn't thrilled with it. I wanted our players to get as much out of this endorsement as they could, but I didn't want them to have to sign their lives away either.

I didn't care how fantastic the numbers looked on paper. No one should be handcuffed into exclusivity with one sponsor. That type of situation had no way to go but down. Yet another lesson I'd learned from my clever husband. He knew how to see the shit hidden within a field of flowers.

Our players needed and deserved to have the freedom to accept other endorsements while playing in the NFL. Most of them had families to provide for, and let's face it, their careers as professional athletes wouldn't last forever.

The music switched over to one of my favorite Marley songs, "Is

This Love." As my hips swayed to the music and my lips hummed the beat, I rested my elbows on the kitchen island and started drafting an email with my suggestions.

To: Wes.Lancaster@Mavericks.com
From: Georgia.Brooks@Mavericks.com

Wes,

    Honestly, their offer—numbers-wise—looks great, but I'm not pleased with the exclusivity for two years bit. Our guys deserve better. I dkmlfjiortwu4389

"Eeeeeep!" I shouted, fingers thumping against the keys.

Large, cool hands already had my dress up to my waist, leaving my bare ass exposed.

"No panties? I approve, Mrs. Brooks," Kline whispered against my skin as his lips peppered kisses down my body. "I swear, your ass is like a gun to my head. There aren't any other possibilities. I *have* to please it for my own survival."

"*Kline,*" I said as I attempted to turn around, but his hands gripped my hips, holding me in place.

"Shh," he admonished, lips still on my skin. "This conversation doesn't involve you." He kneeled behind me, hands gripping my legs and nudging them apart. "It involves my mouth," he murmured, tongue sliding up my inner thigh. "And your delicious pussy." He emphasized the statement by grabbing my ass cheeks and burying his face against me. "And payment for lunch services rendered."

"Oh. *Fuck. Me,*" I moaned, head falling back as Kline ate my pussy from behind. My hips bucked forward once his mouth latched on to my clit, tongue swirling my nerves into a frenzy.

"If you want my cock, baby, you're going to have to wait," he instructed while slipping a finger inside of me. "Because, for the next hour, by your demand, I'm only interested in fucking this perfect cunt with my tongue." I could feel him smile against the skin of my ass. "Or until you come. Which one do you think will happen first?"

"Good God," I whimpered. My body trembled from the intense sensations, tingling and suction and the most delicious burn. And then my hips started rotating with his movements, my climax building at an insanely fast pace. My hands tried to find leverage, fingers banging across the keys of my laptop until I found the edge of the counter to hold on for dear life.

Because holy hell, this was one crazy fucking ride, and my husband wasn't slowing down for anything. Nothing would keep him from getting his fill.

His devious mouth got me off quickly as he knelt on the floor and ate me out from behind.

It wasn't until he was standing, chest pressed against my back, cock hard and already a few inches deep, that I finally remembered I was supposed to be pissed at him.

"I'm mad at you," I breathed, glancing over my shoulder to meet his hooded eyes.

"Still?" he asked, sliding in the rest of the way with one hard, deep thrust.

I moaned.

Fuck, that feels so good. But you're outraged, remember?
You're so mad…ohhhhh…yessssss…

He started to pick up the pace, and my moans grew with each drive of his hips forward.

"Benny?"

"Hmmmm," I mumbled, brain too scrambled to form actual words.

"You still mad at me?"

"Yes," I said in a raspy, damn near porn-y voice. If I wasn't so fucking close to getting off again, I would've been disappointed in my lack of control. But my mind was too focused on reaching that body-shaking moment of perfect horny bliss.

"You mind if we fight about it later, baby?" he asked, slowing his pace to a near stop. "Or did you want to do it now?"

"If you stop fucking me, I'll kill you," I threatened as I drove myself fully onto his cock to emphasize the point.

"Fuck, *yes*," he groaned, picking up speed again. "I love it when you get like this. So fucking greedy to get off."

Kline's hands slid up my sides and pulled down the front of my dress, leaving my breasts bared to his skilled touch. The second his fingers pinched my nipples, tugging them in rhythm with his thrusts, I lost all sense of time, space, *volume*. My moans turned guttural, and I just about screamed the whole place down with each pulsing wave of my orgasm.

"Fuck, fuck, *fuuuuuuuck*," Kline growled as he fell over the edge. His movements turned wild and uncontrolled as he rode out his climax.

My lips to God's ears, my husband might actually fuck me to death before this honeymoon is over. Oh, and thank you, God. Thank you for sending me this perfect specimen of a man.

Once my breathing slowed and my mind could finally form coherent thoughts, I realized I was supposed to be peeved at my husband. I started to pull away from him, but his arms were locked around my body like a vise-grip.

"No way, Benny. You're staying right here." He leaned forward, kissing a path across my shoulder blades.

My body trembled. "I'm angry with you," I whispered.

"Liar." I felt his lips turn up at the corners against my skin.

"I am not lying," I retorted.

"Yes, you are," he said, punctuating the statement with a few small thrusts of his hips. His cock was still inside of me, and somehow, still gloriously hard. "You know what I think?"

"What?"

His lips brushed the shell of my ear. "I think you're just acting like you're mad at me. I think you're trying to get me to have crazed-wild-angry sex with you because you're insatiable. You want to have my cock inside of you this entire honeymoon."

Bingo.

"That doesn't sound like something I'd do."

"Of course not." He laughed. "Stay there, baby," he instructed as he slipped out of me.

A few minutes later, after he cleaned up his *mess*, my husband placed me on top of the island. His hair was still wet from his swim, but he had thrown on a pair of khakis, top button undone and revealing my favorite happy trail. His hands caressed my thighs as he leaned forward and placed a soft, sweet kiss against my lips. "Are you sure you still want to fight?"

I shrugged.

His teeth latched on to my bottom lip, tugging gently. "Your body might be trying to say yes, but your eyes say otherwise."

"What do my eyes say?"

"'My husband fucks like a god.'"

Giggles spilled from my lips. "Be careful, Mr. Brooks, your ego is showing."

He grinned. "Did I meet the requirements of the contract?"

I nodded. "There's a chicken Caesar salad in the fridge."

"I. Love. You," he said, each word punctuated by playful kisses before he headed for the food.

Pulling my laptop on top of my thighs, I tapped my finger against the mouse, and the screen came to life. A new email from Wes was sitting in my inbox.

To: Georgia.Brooks@Mavericks.com
From: Wes.Lancaster@Mavericks.com

Georgia,

    This email started out strong but ended…*oddly*. I have a feeling I don't want to know the details, but I agree with your initial comment about disliking the exclusivity. We'll keep this contract in negotiations until we get our guys the offer they deserve. Tell Kline I said hello.

Wes Lancaster

President and Chief Executive Officer

New York Mavericks

National Football League

I blushed from head to toe. It was one thing for Wes, my boss, to be one of my husband's best friends, but it was another thing for him to *know* I was writing emails while being sexed by my husband.

"Thanks a lot," I muttered as Kline sat down at the breakfast bar, placing his plate beside my thighs.

"Thanks for what?" he asked around a mouthful of salad.

"Your sneak-attack made me send a half-written email to Wes." I held my laptop in front of his eyes, pointing to the message I'd inadvertently sent. "And now he probably thinks I'm just typing up emails while you're fucking me."

"Serves him right," Kline responded with annoyance. "If he doesn't want sexually flawed responses from you, he shouldn't be sending my wife contracts while she's on her honeymoon."

My earlier concerns about my husband not taking my busy work schedule very well had just been confirmed. Sure, his reaction was mild compared to most, but Kline wasn't a lose his temper kind of guy. *That* reaction, albeit, not all that impressive, was him showing his dislike for the situation.

"Oh, I almost forgot to tell you," he said after taking a big gulp of water. "Your mom sent a package. It was sitting on our deck when I got back from my swim."

"Shit," I muttered. "I'm not sure I want to open it."

Kline grinned, knowing full well my mother wasn't known for sending care packages filled with food or gifts from Target.

I hopped off the island and moved toward the deck, where a large cardboard box sat beside the opened doors. The box was made out to Mr. and Mrs. Brooks with the resort's address below it. The sender? *Dr. Crazypants.*

"How in the hell did she manage to get a package to us in Bora Bora? I avoided giving her our hotel information for this very reason."

"She's tenacious."

I huffed out a laugh. "Yeah, she could give you a run for your money in that department."

My fingers removed the tape, and hesitantly, I pried open the cardboard flaps.

"For fuck's sake," I groaned.

"Toys?" Kline asked enthusiastically, standing behind me and peering over my shoulder. He may not have needed the assistance, but my mother's generosity never failed him in entertainment value.

Inside? Three bottles of Anal-Eze—otherwise known as desensitizing lube—four butt plugs in various sizes, and a bunch of other freaky shit I didn't even want to know how to use.

"My mom is a fucking lunatic."

"Well, it's safe to say she's pro-anal," Kline added, amused.

CHAPTER 6

New York, Thursday, April 20th, Afternoon

Cassie

"I can't believe you lost their cat!" I shouted, stomping my foot against the pavement of the sidewalk. We'd been walking in circles, covering what felt like every square inch of Central Park and the ten blocks surrounding Georgia and Kline's. And even though Thatch had suggested we comb the apartment building first, I just *knew* with the way that little fucker enjoyed licking himself on a daily basis, he hadn't wasted any time hanging around, and was probably out looking for pussy in the streets.

Thatch stopped in his tracks and turned to face me. God, he was tall. And big. As he moved closer, I realized just how huge he really was—at least six five and every damn inch of him was framed with big, delicious, he-should-be-naked-all-the-time kind of muscles.

His brown eyes shone in the sunlight as one eyebrow quirked up, and a knowing smile curved the line of his lips, highlighting the dark scruff covering his strong jaw. He was about a week's worth of growth from having an actual beard.

"I lost their cat?" he questioned, visibly amused. "The ol' Thatch film roll shows the cat sneaking out when I was holding back a certain someone who was about to go Fight Club on an elderly woman."

"She was not elderly." I rolled my eyes. "She was like fifty, tops."

He laughed, loud and hearty. I kind of hated the way that laugh forced my focus to his lips. They were thick, full, and downright kissable. "Her name is Mrs. Thomas, and she is five years younger than Kline's grandmother, Marylynn."

Well, *shit*. I guess she was a little older than I thought. Whatever. The bitch—*nice, elderly broad*—had asked for it. I mean, she'd stepped out of her apartment and basically said I wasn't classy. *Pffffft*. I was the classiest bitch I knew. And if I wasn't, I was definitely the *Cassiest*, and that was close-e-fucking-nough.

"How do *you* know who that lady was?"

"Because I know everything, honey." He tapped the side of his head and flashed one of his signature winks. "If it can be seen, I'm seeing it, and anything I can get a hand in, I do." His eyes burned with innuendo and confidence. "It's about time you started figuring that out."

"I swear to God, if you wink at me or another horny admirer on the street *one more fucking time,* I will cut your nuts off."

He laughed, *again,* and then his eyes honed in on my chest. "Ah, don't be jealous. I've been a one-girl-at-a-time kind of a guy since last Thursday. And after the conversation I had with your tits, you're the number one girl on my list."

Christ. This guy. He was maybe the biggest flirt I'd ever met. *Besides me.*

I pushed my braless chest out, knowing full well my nipples were nearly poking holes through my T-shirt. "These tits? They do it for you, baby?" I purred.

"Fuck. Yes." He nodded and swayed toward me like a huge tree in the breeze.

I ran my finger between my cleavage and then back up, crooking it toward him.

He followed, *like a fucking puppy*, until we were chest-to-chest. His gaze met mine, and I flashed him a smile that said, "I want you."

Thatch took that as a *hell yes*, his face morphing to something way more serious than I was expecting.

His mouth closed in on mine, and that's when I dropped the seductive act. Both of my hands reached out, and my fingers found his nipples through his shirt. With both index fingers and thumbs working as a team, I pinched and twisted those babies with all of my might. Probably hard enough to leave bruises.

"Ah, hell!" he shouted, jumping away from me while slapping my hands away in the process. "What the fuck was that for?"

I shrugged and bit my bottom lip. "I thought you liked it rough."

"*What?*" His large hands covered his chest while his face turned to a grimace. "You are literally the craziest woman I've ever met."

"It's about time you started figuring that out." I tossed his earlier words back at him. "And maybe you'll think twice the next time you feel like perving out over my fantastic rack."

"Maybe if you'd worn a bra, I wouldn't be so tempted. Your nipples have been saluting me, *and every other motherfucker* in this city, since we left the apartment."

I glanced down and couldn't exactly disagree. The only reason I wasn't wearing a bra was because Walnuts decided to use my bag as a litter box and Georgia's bras were about three sizes too small. My boobs were big, they had always been big, and though I may have been the type to show some skin, I had never set a precedent for trying to poke people's eyes out with my nipples.

"Okay, since you're basically pathetic and can't stop staring at my boobs, we need to run to my apartment so I can change."

"Thank fuck," he mumbled, following my lead toward the street.

Five minutes and one ear-piercing whistle from Thatch's lips later, we were sitting in a cab, heading toward Chelsea.

"Do you make a habit of prancing around with your tits out like that all the time? And if yes, why don't we hang out more?"

"All the time," I lied. "And we don't hang out because I can't do that around you unless I feel like looking at your boner all day."

"Which you obviously do. So no problem there."

"You wish."

"I don't wish, honey. Ever. I do, and I get—always. If you continue to do that around me, I will propose marriage to your tits, and you can bet your sweet pussy they'll accept."

"They accept nothing less than eight inches and a four-carat pink diamond engagement ring."

He winked. "Good thing I'm packing more than eight, then."

More than eight? I tilted my head as my eyes moved to the crotch of his slacks. I wanted to call bullshit, but I wasn't actually sure I *could* call bullshit.

Fuck it. No use wondering. I reached my hand out toward his lap until it met his zipper. My fingers wrapped around his dick in a viselike grip, assessing the size and girth through his pants. "*Is he a show-er or a grower?*" I silently wondered, but I was quickly denied any further exploration when Thatch shrieked the cabbie's and my ears off.

"What the fuck?" he asked, covering his thick, semi-aroused cock with his large hand.

And just FYI, it was most definitely thick, *and he wasn't lying. That man had a lot of inches, and judging by the half-chub state I managed to get him in, he still had* more *inches to go.*

"First off, that was payback for the boob grab from earlier. Secondly, you can't say shit like that and not expect me to ask questions."

"*Ask questions?*" he said through an incredulous laugh. "Cass, you didn't ask shit. You fucking grabbed my dick and—." He stopped midsentence and then quickly changed his tune. With both hands held away from his lap, he nodded toward the crotch of his pants. "You know what? Go ahead, honey. Ask all the questions you want."

I laughed at his forwardness. This man could give me a run for my money in the over-sharer department. "You're practically gagging over the possibility of grabbing my tits again."

"You have no fucking idea how much."

"Don't mind me," the cabbie interjected with a thick, New York accent. "I won't even charge extra, dollface," he offered with a smirk in the rearview mirror.

I glanced toward the front of the cab, finding the laminated copy of our driver's New York license displayed on the dashboard, and just barely saw Thatch's eyes narrow in my peripheral vision. "Maybe next time, Paul," I teased before hooking a thumb right in front of my giant companion's face. "I got naked in front of this guy once, and I'll never make that mistake again."

"Take it back," Thatch demanded, his nosiness over my cab-driver relations forgotten.

"Consider my curiosity curbed, Thatcher. You can go ahead and put your boner away."

"I can't wait for the day when you eat those words." His grin was all cocky and self-assured.

"Don't hold your breath," I taunted.

I was so totally full of shit, by the way. My curiosity wasn't curbed; it was at an all-time high after getting my grope on. Thatcher Kelly was packing, and my puss-ay was practically begging for a ride on his baloney pony.

"Oh, yeah?" he asked.

"Yeah!"

"Your words are going to continue to feel hollow until you actually take your hand off my dick, Pinocchio."

I looked down to see he was right. My small hand sat firm and full in the crotch of his pants.

How the fuck did that thing get back there?

"Do you think they have one of those microchips on Walter?" Thatch asked as we got off the elevator and moved toward my apartment door.

"Micro-whats? What are you talking about?" I slid the key in the lock and opened the door.

"Micro*chips*," he answered, following me inside and shutting the door with a quiet click. "You know, when the vet uses a needle to place a little chip under your pet's skin. The chip has a unique number on it, and if your pet gets lost—" He stopped, assessing the confused look on my face. "You have no idea what I'm talking about, do you?"

"Not a clue." I shook my head, walking down the hall and into my bedroom. "I did hear the words *if your pet gets lost*, though, so I'm kind of hoping you're on to something."

"You've never heard of microchips before?" Thatch stayed hot on my heels, seemingly making himself right at home and plopping his fine ass onto my bed.

"Um, no. But that's probably because I don't have any pets that would require one," I muttered, rummaging through my armoire and pulling a white lace bra out of the drawer.

"Have you ever owned a pet?"

I turned to face him, hand on my hip. "What does that have to do with anything?"

"You just don't really seem like the pet-owning type." He shrugged, sliding his giant hands behind his head. His biceps flexed from the movement, making those delicious muscles pop and protrude for my appreciative eyes.

I had always had a thing for biceps. Big, thick, muscular arms were my jam. And for the love of porn GIFs, did this man have some glorious fucking biceps. I wanted to pet them, caress them, rub my tongue, tits, and pussy all over them.

Yeah, I don't understand the whole dynamics of rubbing my vagina on his arms either, but I thought it, so there you have it.

"Cass?" His voice pulled me from my bicep-humping daydream.

"Huh?"

He flashed a knowing smirk in my direction. "You never answered my question."

"Obviously, it didn't seem that important to me. Otherwise, I would've answered," I retorted as I Houdini'd my bra on without removing my shirt. I honestly didn't know what Thatch would do if he got another glance at my bare chest.

"You can touch them, you know." He flexed one meaty arm and winked. "You can touch any fucking thing you want."

Obviously, Mr. Ego hadn't missed my admiring perusal of his arms.

I sighed. "Just because I was appreciating your fuck-hot body does *not* mean I want to play hide the salami. I'd need a blood test before I even thought about letting you inside my tight, hot pussy."

"Prove it, honey."

"Prove what?"

He patted the empty spot on the bed beside him. "I need to

know exactly how tight and hot before I provide you with a vial of my blood and medical records."

"Get over yourself," I said with a laugh. "And what did you ask me before?"

"Have you ever had a pet?"

Childhood memories flooded my brain. "Like, as a kid?"

"Yeah, did you have a dog or cat or even a goldfish?"

I nodded, picturing Dad running through the backyard. "As a matter of fact, I did have a pet growing up."

He waited a good thirty seconds before saying, "Okay, care to share?"

"When I was eight, I had a mini-pig. He was the coolest motherfucking pet in my neighborhood. I loved that pig. Probably more than my baby brother, Sean."

"What was his name?"

"Dad."

His eyebrows scrunched together. *"Dad?"*

"Yeah, his name was Dad. Dad, the mini-pig. He was white with—" I started to respond, but Thatch held his hand up, laughter spilling from his lips.

"Hold up. Your pig's name was Dad?"

"Uh, yeah." My right eyebrow rose on my forehead, high and annoyed. "How many times do I have to tell you my pig's name?"

"Who named him?"

"Me. I named him. He was my pig." I stared at him, frustrated by his interrogation. "English is your first language, right?"

He chuckled at that. "You realize how fucking absurd and downright hilarious it is that you, little toothless, pigtail-wearing-Cassie, named her pig Dad, right?"

"He looked like a Dad. And I was never innocent enough to pull off pigtails."

"Fuck, you're fantastic." A giant grin consumed his face. "What happened to Dad?"

"My mom got tired of him constantly tearing up the house, so they sent him to a farm."

"A farm, farm? Or like 'a farm'?" he asked, gesturing quotation marks with his fingers.

I squinted. "I don't understand the difference. I thought a farm was a fucking farm."

He slowly tilted his head to the side, assessing my incredulous expression. After a few seconds, he merely smiled and got off my bed, walking around my bedroom and getting all up in my personal shit.

I followed his big-ass feet across the room, yanking a picture frame from his hands. "Not so fast, Thatcher. What other kind of farm are you talking about?"

For a fraction of a second, I watched his eyes go wide before he schooled his expression into one that was irritatingly neutral.

And then, it clicked. The bastard was insinuating that my mom had Dad offed. He hadn't been—I'd checked, and had even made my mother get pictures of Dad with his new farm family. Well, two could play that game. I'd make Thatch rethink opening his big fucking mouth before I was through with him. Good thing I'd always been a *fantastic* actress.

"Oh, my God!" My hand went to my mouth. "You don't think my—"

"No," he backtracked, eyes wide and head shaking adamantly.

I almost wanted to drop the act when I saw the distressed look on his face. *Almost.*

"That's not what I said. I'm sure your parents sent Dad to a real farm. A really nice farm. I bet Dad had the time of his life at that farm. I bet he was a wild man, doing crazy pig shit and frolicking in the fields. Maybe you ate a lot of ham that month, but I'm sure it was a coincidence."

Ham. It took a whole lot of willpower not to burst out into laughter. Even when he was trying to be serious, he couldn't help himself. The man was sarcastic to his core, and it gave me a very odd sense of déjà vu.

"Oh. My. God!" I shoved his shoulder hard, forcing him to take a step back. "You think my mom had Dad killed?!"

His eyes transformed from playful to panicked.

"No. No. That's not what I think. I think he grew old on that happy, beautiful farm. I bet Dad died doing what he loved, rolling around in shit and pulling some serious piggy tail."

"I can't believe this," I said, staring off into space and putting on my best distraught look. "I can't believe my mom killed Dad. I feel like my entire childhood is a lie. My whole life is one big fucking lie. Thanks a lot, Thatch!" I stabbed him in the chest with my index finger. "You have ruined *everything*."

"Fuck." He ran a hand through his hair. "I'm sure Dad is still alive. I bet that fucker's gonna live to be a hundred!"

"Shut up. Just. Shut. Up." I turned away from him, fighting the smile threatening to cover my entire face, and threw myself onto my mattress. "This whole time I thought Dad was happy with another family on a farm, when in reality, he was dead." My voice was muffled in my pillows. "Dad was dead, and no one even fucking knew about it. My mom fucking had Dad offed because, apparently, he was too much of a hassle."

A soft chuckle hit my ears, and I turned onto my back, finding Thatch vibrating with silent laughter. The expression on his face—a fine mix of hilarity and constipation—almost made me break.

"Are you laughing?" My lips burned as I tried to hide my amusement with feigned disgust.

"Definitely not. That'd be a real asshole thing to do," he muttered, trying like hell to fight a smile. He assessed my face and started to grin. "Wait a minute..." He paused, pointing a finger at my face. "Are you fucking with me?"

"Are you insinuating I'm not upset about Dad?"

He nodded. "That's exactly what I'm saying. And by the look of that smile trying to swallow your face, I'd say I'm right. You look like the fucking Joker." He laughed, shaking his head. "It actually scares me how good you are at acting. I feel bad for every motherfucker that's fallen inside your trap. You should come with a warning label, honey."

Even though he was one-hundred-percent correct, I still grabbed my TV remote from the nightstand and chucked it at him for having the audacity to accuse me of being a lot to handle. I *was*, but only *I* got to say I was high-maintenance.

Unfortunately, Thatch was a lot quicker than he looked, crouching down, and giving the remote nowhere else to go but straight at my window. It cracked and shattered with an impressive screech, glass flying onto the hardwood floor like confetti.

Well, *fuck*.

He straightened from his crouched position and assessed the damage. His fingers running along the broken glass and noting the giant hole in the center.

Thatch turned around, facing me. "I'll take the blame for breaking the news to you about Dad's death, but this—" he gestured a thumb over his shoulder "—this one's on you, crazy."

I sighed. "Son. Of. A. Bitch."

And that was how I had managed to get Thatcher Kelly shirtless and sweaty, hammering nails into a piece of plywood that covered my broken window.

"Honestly, Cass, if you wanted a striptease, all you had to do was ask. I would've obliged, and you wouldn't have to replace a window." He glanced over his shoulder, smirking.

I was lying on my belly, chin resting in my hands, and enjoying the show from the comfort of my bed. A few rogue droplets of sweat slid down his back, bumping over the beautiful dips and valleys of his muscular form. Damn, this man had to put some serious hours in at the gym to look that good.

"Did you hear me?" he asked, lining up another nail against the wood. "Next time, let's avoid all of the menial labor and focus both of our energies on something more entertaining. Something that involves your tits and me in a deep, mouth-to-nipple conversation."

"Why are you still talking?" I took a sip from the straw inside my can of Coke. "You're supposed to be standing there, hammering your wood, and looking pretty. I'm not paying you for small talk."

"Pretty sure you're not paying me at all," he pointed out. "Your crazy ass broke the window, and now I'm stuck putting up a temporary solution until you can get someone in here to replace it."

"Meh, those are just minor details at this point."

"Okay. Here's the deal," he said, lining up another nail. "Wrap those gorgeous lips of yours around my cock, and we'll call it even."

"*Slut,*" I responded through a cough.

"I never said dirty talk was a requirement, but if that's what gets you off, I guess I can roll with it." He glanced over his shoulder and waggled his eyebrows in my direction.

"You know," I responded, tapping my chin. "Considering I'm a fan of sucking cock, I probably would've gone for it. But since you lost Walter, and we've yet to find Satan himself, I'm gonna have to pass."

"Shit. I almost forgot about that goddamn cat," Thatch muttered.

"Yeah, I kind of did too," I said, eyes still fixated on his biceps as he hammered in the last nail. I was starting to think we were terrible friends to Kline and Georgie. I probably should have been out searching for Walnuts rather than lounging around, watching Thatch's big muscles at work.

It was definitely time to resume our search. No way in hell

could I let Georgia come home to her cat missing.

I got up from my bed and headed for the hallway. "Move those fucking clown feet into my bathroom and get cleaned up. Time's a wastin' on finding The Asshole." I called over my shoulder.

A few feet into the hallway, I heard Thatch mutter, "Jesus Christ. That little cocksucker. Not even my cat, and he's ruining *everything*."

CHAPTER 7

Thatch

"**D**on't you think we should actually search the *apartment building* in which he vanished *before* the rest of Manhattan?" I asked for the *second* time today.

Crazy Cassie had been convinced immediately after Walter's disappearing act that he'd up and, I don't know, fucking teleported himself to the other side of Central Park. She'd dragged me out onto the sidewalk, and led by the helpful direction of her tits, I'd followed right along on a roller coaster ride straight into hell. Up and down the sidewalks of the park, from one side to the other and back again, a Twilight Zone cab ride, and a little light manual labor at her apartment later, and here I was, about to follow her into the depths of Manhattan fitness and fornication *again*.

I guess that makes me the crazy one.

"Would you stop contradicting every fucking thing I say? Use that beanstalk body of yours and search the surrounding area."

Fed up, I pulled her to a stop with the hand she was dragging me by. "I'm going back to search the building, and if I don't find him, I'm calling Kline."

"Thatcher—"

"No, Cass. Stay out here and search if you want, but you'll never find Walnuts in the bevy of strays combing Central Park. God, for all we know, the little prick has a key to their apartment and is halfway through his afternoon bath in the middle of their goddamn bed."

"*Shit!*" she yelled, her face falling as she started running in the direction we had come, shoving people out of the way as she went.

"What?" I asked, breaking into a jog to keep up.

"The door!" she shrieked. "We left the door to their apartment open!"

Oh, *fuck.*

Yeah, safe bet they weren't going to be asking us to watch their apartment or their cat again.

My legs were twice the length of hers, so I passed her easily, sprinting through the crowded sidewalk. I slammed through the door, nodding at the doorman as I went, and thanking *fuck* their building had one.

Too impatient to wait for the elevator, I took the stairs three at a time. Fourteen stories up with sweat pouring like a fucking faucet from my temples, I finally burst through the stairwell door and out into their hallway.

The door was open just like Cass had said, so I said a silent prayer I hadn't just deprived my best friend and his new bride of all their belongings.

Shoving the door as I went, I slid to a stop just inside and examined the open floor plan with manic eyes. All the furniture seemed to be in place, and nothing of value stood out as missing, but I hadn't kept an actual fucking inventory list either.

I'd just started to take a full breath when a tap on my shoulder sent me into a near seizure.

Cassie spoke as if nothing was amiss. "Stuff's all here, but no devil cat. The door was closed, by the way. Whoops."

I put a hand to my forehead and tried to stop the nearly brain-piercing urge to strangle her.

"What took you so long?" she went on, having beaten me up here by taking the elevator.

White-hot rage consumed every cubic inch of my insides, but I tried my best to tamp it down.

Is this what an aneurysm feels like?

"Hey, Thatcher, you okay?" she asked, her face turning serious as I sank to the floor and rubbed at the tension in my temples. Her bra-covered breasts pushed against the fabric of her T-shirt as she sat down beside me.

How in the fuck did I still find this crazy asshole woman attractive? What was wrong with me?

"Jesus Christ," I mumbled, scrubbing at my eyes and hoping they had some kind of link to my actions. "I want to donate my brain to science."

"Huh?"

"Like the football players are doing for concussions. I think this would be worthwhile research too." As my head fell back to the wall behind me, she nudged me roughly with one of her feet.

"I don't even know what you're talking about right now, but stop it," she demanded. "You're scaring me, and it's pissing me off."

I turned my head and looked into her eyes to find them *actually* angry, spitting blue flames and making the end of her nose pull slightly askew. She straddled the line between angelic and evil too easily. She foiled that boundary with the mystifying mix of her peaches and cream skin and powerful, knowing eyes.

Too wild to be innocent, too authentic to be wicked.

Her light pink lips pursed, and without a thought, mine were on them. They acted on their own, begging for an invitation from her or me, or both of us, to take it further. One moment bled into the next without thought or action until her lips moved under mine. Not far and not open, but not away either.

Stunned, I pulled back. I couldn't understand it, but something in me didn't want to hear her say no—so I said it for her.

"Thank fuck," I said, a rough rasp lingering in the edges of my voice. "I finally found a way to shut you up."

The vivid blue of her eyes clouded by derision, she jumped to standing. Though they were marred, they were still resoundingly powerful, chaining me to them. Even knowing her chest must have bounced with the movement, my gaze never left the confounded lines of her face. It was so out of character; I didn't even recognize myself.

"Don't ever kiss me again without permission," she whispered shakily. The rough edge of her command cut like a knife. All traces of superficial playfulness had disappeared, and the look in her eyes burned through several layers of flesh until it met my soul.

Some kind of nerve had been frayed, and I wasn't sure I was a talented enough surgeon to execute the repair. The only option was to move on, and the only tactic I knew how to employ was avoidance.

I climbed to my feet. "Let's search for Walter one more time. Here, inside the apartment, and around this floor. If we don't find him in the next thirty minutes or so, I'll call Kline."

"That deadbeat isn't going to care! Georgie cares. Fuck, she's gonna be mad."

"Don't worry," I comforted her but didn't move closer. "Kline gives no fucks about Walter, but he gives all kinds of fucks about Georgia. He'll hire a fucking private detective if he has to."

"A cat detective?" she asked as she considered my words, tilting her head to the side and grinning just enough to look normal again.

I shrugged and breathed out a sigh of relief. "Yeah. If there are cat burglars, there must be cat detectives, right?"

"You're an idiot."

"Yeah." We didn't agree on much, but on that, we were on the same fucking page.

I was thinking things I shouldn't be thinking. Things that would probably never happen. Things I wasn't even sure I wanted to happen.

And that made me the goddamn king of royally fucked.

CHAPTER 8

Bora Bora, Thursday, April 20th, Afternoon

Kline

I glanced through the open bathroom door to the steam coming out of the shower and back down to the screen of my phone to confirm the name on the incoming call said what I thought it did.

It fucking did.

With a touch of the green phone icon and a frustrated groan, I answered and didn't mince words. "You, Cassie, Wes, or Walter better be dead or in the process of getting that way."

"What if I told you Wes is fine, Cassie's crazy, I almost died, and the cat is missing?" Thatch said in my ear without pause.

"Shit." The piercing pain of aggravation made me squeeze the bridge of my nose between my thumb and forefinger.

"Yeah," he confirmed.

I turned to face away from the bathroom and paced the space in front of the bed.

"The first three I understand, but how in the fuck did we arrive at the fourth? Walter is the bane of my existence, but other than being sloppy and surly, he's surprisingly easy to watch."

"Well, we thought it happened while I was having a conversation with Cassie's tits—and seriously, we'll have to have another talk about that later—but it actually happened while she was threatening to go all Fight Club with your neighbor."

"It's actually painful to be friends with you right now."

Exasperated laughter pulsed in my ear. "I'm picking up on that. You've got a seriously heavy aura pouring through the phone lines right now."

"You know what comes through right after my aura?" I asked.

"Something tells me I don't wanna know, but at the same time, I have to know."

"My hand. To fucking strangle you."

"Kline—"

"I'm on my honeymoon right now," I pointed out the obvious. "A vacation specifically designed for constant sex with my insanely hot wife. And you and fucking Wes won't stop interrupting it."

I sat down on the edge of the bed and glanced toward the bathroom again.

"I don't know about Wes, but this is my first and final time, dude. I just want to know if the cat's got a tracking chip in it."

I wrapped a hand around my throat, dropped my head back, and closed my eyes. "I'm not completely sure, but my mom would know. She did all of his vet stuff."

"Thank fuck," he muttered. He actually sounded worn-out and weird. But I didn't care. I planned to save all of my energy for exponentially more pleasurable activities, and I refused to let my tendency to *care* get in the way of that.

"She's also likely to make your life a living hell if you speak with her directly about her missing, beloved cat," I advised. "Your best bet is to talk to Bob."

Thatch chuckled. "I don't know why you decided to show leniency toward me by telling me that, but thank you. I can only handle one irrational woman at a time."

"You're welcome. And you owe me." I stood from the bed again and looked out at the turquoise water. If it weren't for the sun, it might have looked like it went on forever.

He sighed. "I'm completely unsure how my watching your cat has ended in me owing you *another* favor, but I don't even care. As long as this day ends without bloodshed or blue balls, I'll count it as a very difficult win."

My eyebrows pinched together, and I turned to the sound of Georgie in the bathroom door. "I don't know, I don't want to know, I don't need to know. Just take care of it," I said in vague dismissal.

Thatch laughed yet again in my ear. "Break it to her easy, K. Probably best if you mumble it while your mouth is otherwise occup—"

"Bye," I interrupted, pulling the phone from my ear and hanging up before he could say anything else.

"Who was that?" Georgie asked, cinching her towel tighter around her body. This definitely wasn't the way I wanted to start the second part of our day. I had a special dinner planned, and I wanted my wife nothing but sated, sassy, and seductive. If she knew about Walter, all of those things would go straight to hell.

"Thatch," I muttered, turning around to set my phone on the nightstand and gathering my thoughts on how to handle this.

"Is everything okay? Is Cass okay? Did Walter kill her?" she asked rapid-fire, immediately on edge. I had to smile about the last question.

"Did he *kill* her?" I asked with a snicker. "You know, Benny, I'm searching my brain, but all I can seem to remember is you defending him. Telling people what a sweetheart he is. Why would you think affable little Walter would do anything other than love and protect your best friend?"

Her eyes narrowed, and a foot rotated out into her fighting stance. I bit my lip to curtail a smile. "This isn't about Walter. This is about Cassie. I love her dearly, but she's really good at instigating and infuriating. It wouldn't take much of her to make our softhearted cat turn."

I shook my head and charged her, scooping her into my arms and smelling the fresh scent of her neck. She squealed but wrapped her arms around my shoulders. I tugged her towel free and spoke at the same time. "God, you're good. Are you sure you can't come back to work with me?"

She pulled back, pushing me off her gently and raising a brow. "Kline—"

"I know, I know. You're happy where you are. I get it," I surrendered, pulling her immediately back into my arms.

"Kline, we should talk about this. It's obviously bothering you."

"I don't want to talk about it," I told her honestly. "I want to ignore it and everything else but you and us and our honeymoon."

She put a hand to my jaw and looked into my eyes.

"Does it bother me?" I went on. "Yeah. Obviously, it does. But not like you're thinking, and not to the point that I can't put on my fucking big-boy pants and get over it. When our honeymoon is over, we'll talk about it more. Make the compromises we need to. But for now, the only aggression I want between the two of us is between the sheets, on the deck, in the pool, in the shower—any-goddamn-where as long as our clothes are off and our bodies are as close as we can get them."

"Baby," she whispered, wrapping her tan, bare legs around my waist and squeezing tight.

"Let's start now, Benny. Argue with me the only way I like it."

"Why are you so good with words?" she replied softly as she pulled her body closer into mine.

"Business," I told her with a wink. She laughed. "And to use as a tool to woo you."

"I'm wooed," she responded with a smirk. "Whatever will you use your mouth for now?"

Reaching around and under her ass, I sank the tips of my fingers right in between her legs and nibbled at her shoulder. "I was going to use it to get your pussy ready for me, but she's already all set."

"Um," she mumbled through a moan. "What *is* ready? I mean, can you ever *really* be ready?"

"You're right," I agreed as I laid her gently on the bed and shoved my boxer briefs down my legs and stepped out of them. I stroked my cock from root to tip and back again before running the fingers of my other hand straight up the middle of her wet pussy. "There's no way she's ready for this," I taunted. "My tongue is gonna tease you until you think you're prepared. That sound good, Rose?"

She always blushed when I called her that, and when she was completely bare, the color didn't stop at her cheeks.

Down to my knees, I scooped her legs up and over my shoulders and buried my face right in the middle. Her hips chased my tongue, and I pushed forward to make sure they didn't have to go far.

"Mmm," I moaned, deeply sucking in all of her sweetness. "My little flower tastes good."

"God, Kline," she hummed.

She was magnificent in all of her pleasure, licking lips and greedy hips moving at a constant pace. She wanted more and less, and I intended to give her everything she wanted, even if it was impossible. The sun-darkened color of her skin made her eyes stand out, and every second I spent looking at her pussy, I could feel them on me. Watching, begging—fucking forcing me to work her harder, faster, slower, softer. Everything she asked for, I felt it, and you couldn't convince me there was any better feeling in the world than being this in tune with another person.

"Come on, baby," I pushed while I teased her ass with my thumb and her clit with my tongue. "Get *ready*. Get fucking soaked."

I pumped two fingers in and out of her and she clenched around me, but she did it silently. Lost in her euphoria, her head fell back and her mouth fell open. I hated not seeing her eyes, but the line of her throat, the spasm in her thighs, and the grip of her hand in my hair told me every goddamn thing I ever wanted or needed to know.

"Ready?" I asked, climbing to my feet and wrapping a hand around the base of my aching dick.

She demanded my arousal with her eyes and my heart with her words. "Always."

Always.

CHAPTER 9

Bora Bora, Friday, April 21ˢᵗ, Afternoon

Georgia

I stirred from my afternoon doze on the quiet beach as strong hands kneaded into my back. Glancing over my shoulder, I found Kline kneeling beside my prone form, holding a bottle of sunscreen in one hand as he squirted more lotion into his open palm.

I took a minute to enjoy the view. His body gloriously bared, only a pair of swim trunks sat low on his trim waist. He was fresh off a swim, dark hair slicked back with several rogue droplets of water slipping down his chest to the muscles of his abdomen, and if his hands kept up this delicious torture, he wouldn't be the only one wet.

"How long have I been asleep?" I asked, voice raspy from yet another nap under the sun.

In my defense, I was tired from last night's exertions that included more than one round of hot honeymoon sex. Before that, we had dinner on the beach, with Kline hand-feeding me through most of it. Yeah, there was no denying my husband was one swoo-

ny bastard. He wooed me right out of my panties and onto his or-
gasm-inducing cock.

"Probably an hour," he said, a smile in his voice. His hands
made a slow descent down my back, rubbing soft circles into my
skin. "This is becoming a habit, Benny girl. You falling asleep by
noon."

"It's all your fault," I muttered, turning my head to the side and
resting it on my folded hands.

"My fault?" he asked while his devious fingers slid my bikini
bottoms out of the way.

"Uh-huh." I shut my eyes and swallowed a moan.

His large hands gripped my ass and *pretended* to apply sunscreen.

"Pretty sure I don't need sun protection there."

"I'm thorough, Georgie." He was undeterred, still groping my
body in the name of preventing sunburn.

"This feels less like you applying sunscreen and more like you
trying to get me naked."

He smacked my ass, and I squealed in surprise. When my eyes
met his, I wasn't surprised to find them positively glowing.

"Turn over and let me get the rest of you."

I giggled, turning over onto my back, and my eyes squinted as
the bright sun shone directly into them.

Kline kneeled between my spread legs, hands sliding up my
sides until his fingers stopped to play with the edge of my bikini top.
"Damn, you're fucking beautiful." He rested his elbows beside my
head and placed soft, sweet kisses against my lips. "I could spend
the next fifty years just staring at my gorgeous wife and never have
my fill."

"Fifty years from now, I'll be a lot less gorgeous and a lot more
wrinkled and gray," I said against his persistent mouth.

He leaned back just enough to meet my gaze. "In my eyes, you'll always be the most stunning, tiny, perfect being."

"Even when I'm old?"

"Especially when you're old." He placed a wet, deep kiss against my lips.

See what I mean? Swoony fucking bastard.

His lips rested against mine as he spoke again. "My standards will have lessened, and I'm pretty sure you'll age well."

Hmm…Okay, so maybe he's just a bastard.

Chuckles bounced off my skin as he lost himself in his humor. "Relax, baby. I'm kidding."

"You better be kidding," I mumbled, huffing and puffing on my chair as I pushed him away.

He resumed his sunscreen application, squirting more into his palm and kneading those strong fingers into my belly. "What do you want to do today?"

Hells bells, his hands were an aphrodisiac.

I thought it over, but I didn't have to think hard. "Stay here and let my husband give me the five-star treatment."

He chuckled, waggling his brows. "All of my massages end with happy endings."

"I thought this was sunscreen application?"

"Okay. All activities that include my hands on you end happily." He winked and moved those greedy hands farther up my stomach until they were resting just below the swell of my breasts.

Oh boy, this man was perfect. If he kept it up, I'd start purring like a fucking cat.

Purring like a cat? For some reason, I felt like I'd been down this line of thinking before.

Oh, shit! Cat! The cat!

I sat up abruptly, forcing Kline's hands to fall from my skin.

"Hey, I wasn't done," he responded, hands moving toward me again. They found my ribs and started tickling me into giggling.

"Stop it!" I playfully slapped him away and grabbed my beach bag, rummaging through it in search of my phone.

"You bring some toys to the beach, Benny?"

"No, you kinky bastard," I said through a laugh. I pulled my phone from the bag and held it up for him to see. "I forgot to call Cass and check on Walter."

His expression changed from devilish smirk to something a lot less excited in the span of a heartbeat.

"What's wrong?" I tilted my head to the side, taken aback by his sudden change in mood.

"Kline?"

He grimaced before he spoke. "I need to tell you something."

My nose crinkled involuntarily. "Is everything okay?"

"I talked to Thatch and—"

"Oh, my God!" My hand covered my mouth. "Did something happen? Did something happen to Cass?"

He shook his head. "No, baby. Cassie is fine."

I put my hand to my chest, trying to slow my racing heart. "Don't scare me like that. I thought something terrible happened."

"Baby, Thatch called yesterday to tell me that…" He trailed off, watching me with concerned and cautious eyes. He took a deep breath and then finally added, "Walter got out of the apartment, and they're having a hard time locating him."

"*What?*" My eyes bugged out and I shot to my feet, pointing an accusatory finger in Kline's face. "Walter is missing, and you didn't fucking tell me?!"

His face was a mask of shame and *Ah, shit, yes*, and the combination of the two sent me running for our bungalow.

"Georgia!" I heard him call after me.

But I was at a damn near sprint, racing to get inside and pack my shit. Call me a lunatic, I didn't care. My baby was missing, and I'd be damned if he spent another lonely night in some decrepit alley in New York.

Tears filled my eyes as I pictured him walking the streets, cold, wet, and with no goddamn food.

My husband found me in the bedroom, tossing my suitcase onto the mattress.

"Baby," he said, voice hesitant. "What are you doing?"

"What does it look like I'm doing?" I threw my hands out in front of me in a wild, erratic gesture of *isn't it fucking obvious*. "I'm packing my shit. I need to get home! Walter is missing and cold and wet and lonely and just walking the streets of New York looking for me."

I moved toward the closet to get my clothes, but I stopped in my tracks as my brain started conjuring all of the worst scenarios. "Oh, my God!" I covered my mouth with my hand as a shocked gasp escaped my lungs. "What if he becomes desperate, Kline? What if he has no other choice but to start prostituting himself for food? You know he's not good at making new friends! There's no way he's been accepted by the good crowd. He's probably already addicted to heroin!"

"Georgie," Kline cooed in my ear, arms wrapping around my body and pulling my back into his chest. "I'm sure Walter is fine. You know Maureen. She made sure he has one of those GPS tracking chips. I bet Cass and Thatch have already found him by this point."

"You don't know that! They would've called if they found him." I pushed his arms away and moved into the closet, yanking clothes off the hangers.

Kline was standing by my suitcase when I strode back in with both arms full of sundresses and bikinis.

"Call the airline! We have to get on the next flight out." I threw everything into my suitcase and headed for the bathroom to grab my toiletries.

But my husband stopped my momentum, wrapping his arms around me again and pulling me into a tight bear hug.

"We don't have time for this!"

He kept his hold on me, lifting me into his arms and carrying me into the hallway.

"Put me down!" I tried like hell to get out of his hold as he walked down the stairs, but it was pointless. He was too strong, no matter how much adrenaline I had running through my system.

He sat me down on the kitchen island, stood between my knees, and his hands gripped my thighs to hold me in place. "I need you to take a deep breath and calm down for a minute." His voice should have been calming, but it was just pissing me off more.

"I can't calm down!" I shouted. "Everything is all fucked up! Our cat is missing, and *you* didn't tell me. You lied to me, Kline! I feel like you keep lying to me about a lot of shit."

His eyes turned remorseful at my accusations, but they weren't completely complacent either. "I know I should have told you about Walter, but I didn't want you to panic."

"You told me everything was fine and that Walter was good, but in reality, he's sitting in an alley shooting up heroin!"

"Baby, I—"

"Do *not* baby me." I pointed my index finger at him.

His eyes narrowed, and one thing became clear. Sweet, patient Kline was losing a little of both.

I knew I was probably being a little—okay, *a lot*—irrational, but I couldn't help it. Ever since the whole Rose and Ruck debacle, my husband had made it a point always to be open and honest with me, but lately, he had been doing the opposite. I knew he wasn't happy about my job situation, yet he just kept brushing it off and refusing to discuss it.

But it *was* bothering him. *Big. Time.* And, let's be honest, the fact that it was bothering him was *really* bothering me.

And now, he'd lied to me about the cat. It felt like the icing on the dishonesty cake.

"Georgia," he started to say, but I held up my hand.

"I can't go there right now. I need to call Cassie and see if they've found Walter."

I glanced around the kitchen, but I remembered the last time I had my phone was *before* I had hauled ass to our bungalow. "Shit! I think I left my phone on the beach."

Kline grabbed my bag—that he had obviously carried inside for me—from one of the barstools and reached inside. "Here." He handed the phone to me. "Call Cassie and see if they found Walter."

I didn't even hesitate. Three rings in, I hopped off the island and started to pace.

On the fourth ring, she finally answered. "Helloooooo, Wheorgie! How's Bora Bora? Is Kline at least feeding you between—"

"Did you find Walter?" I asked, too worried to let her ramble any further.

"Uh…I guess Kline told you about that, huh?"

"Did you find my cat?" I snapped.

"He has a tracking device, Georgie. We could find him on the moon with the GPS shit your mother-in-law embedded under his skin."

"Oh, thank God." I breathed a sigh of relief. "I was about one minute away from booking a flight home."

"You were going to leave your honeymoon because the dickhead…was missing?"

"Are you kidding me? My baby was missing! Of course, I was going to fly home to find him!"

"Slow your roll, Susie. No need to make me deaf," she muttered into my ear.

"Is he okay?"

"Uh…yeah…I'm sure he's just fine."

"He's not hurt? Was he scared? I can't believe he was lost and roaming the streets of New York all by himself."

"Walter is one tough little asshole. You have nothing to worry about."

"Will you stay at our apartment for the rest of our trip? I think he could really use the companionship."

"Already planned on it. Sorry to cut this short, but I gotta jet. I've got a shoot in about thirty minutes. I'll call you later, okay?"

"Sounds good. Oh, hey, Cass?

"Yeah?"

"If you lose my cat again, I will kill you."

She scoffed. "You can guarantee I won't lose that little bastard a second time."

"Good."

"Georgia, stop sulking and go blow your husband. Lord knows he probably needs the extra attention after watching you lose your shit."

"I did not lose my shit!"

Kline snorted in the background.

"Sure you didn't." She laughed. "My money says you had half your shit packed and were *already* telling Kline to book a flight."

Jesus, she knew me too fucking well.

"Shut up. Go snap pervy photos of naked men."

"Later, Wheorgie!"

I hung up the call and met Kline's gaze. He was still standing by the island, watching me with uncertainty and unhappiness dulling his blue eyes.

"Everything okay?"

I nodded and tried to collect the scattered pieces of myself. "They found him."

"That's good news."

"Yeah, it is," I agreed.

We just stared at one another, lost in my earlier mania and the deeper issues it'd brought to light. A cloud of hurt feelings and harsh accusations hung over our otherwise blissful honeymoon.

"Well...I guess I better go clean up the disaster area. I'll make us some lunch once I finish, okay?" I called over my shoulder as I walked up the stairs toward our bedroom, hoping to have a few moments to find my way back to five on the emotional scale.

To my surprise, Kline followed me.

He sat on the bed as I started to empty my suitcase. "Come here, sweetheart." When I looked to him but didn't move, he gestured for me to come closer.

The second I was within his reach, he pulled me onto his lap and wrapped his arms around my stomach. His face was pressed against my neck, lips brushing the sensitive spot below my ear. The intimate silence healed half the hurt, but some of it stayed, buried deep.

After a few quiet moments, I whispered, "I'm sorry I went a little crazy before."

Hot, relieved air coated my skin. "I'm sorry I lied to you."

I leaned back, gripping his chin and forcing his eyes to look at mine. "Are you really sorry about that?"

"*Yes.* Of course I am, Ben." His remorseful eyes stared deep into mine.

"What about my job?"

He cocked an eyebrow. "What about your job?"

"Are you going to start being honest with me about how you

really feel about it?"

He sighed and gave me a squeeze. "I'm not happy about the amount of time it will demand from you, but I'll deal."

"I don't think saying you'll deal is a solution, Kline. What if you start resenting me for traveling so much? For being occupied with work too much? Where will that lead us?"

God, the words stung as soon as I said them.

What if my job started to put a giant wedge between us?

We had gotten together in a rush. Too consumed with one another, too deep in love not to dive headfirst into our relationship. We had known each other for a few years, but we hadn't actually been together, been a couple, for all that long.

What if my job strained my marriage?

The mere thought of that awful scenario caused tears to pool in my eyes.

CHAPTER 10

Kline

Seeing tears in her eyes over the possibility of a disillusioned marriage courtesy of a fucking job was the last straw. I'd wanted to maintain our "eat, fuck, cuddle, sleep, be nauseatingly happy" bubble for these two weeks, but the bubble wasn't any fucking good if it hurt her.

And right now? The compartmentalization on my part was very much hurting my sweet wife.

"All right," I declared, picking her up from my lap and setting her down on the edge of the bed. Standing in front of her, I tipped her chin up until her pretty, sad eyes met mine. "Real talk time." She steeled herself for what she thought might come. "First things first, no more tears, okay?"

"Kline—"

"They break my fucking heart, Benny. I can't think of a scenario where I like to see you cry, but I fucking *loathe* it when I'm the cause."

She did her best to stop, as I moved on. The important point wasn't that she actually stop crying; it was that she knew I *wanted* her to.

"How often am I right while you're wrong?" I asked, catching her off guard. I could see at first that she wasn't sure how to answer, but I prompted her to be honest with gentle eyes and a soft smile.

"Not often."

Bingo.

"So not often," I admitted. "I'm completely prepared for the inevitable. With me being the man and you the woman, the rightness ratio in this relationship will always heavily favor you. It's been the way of the world for centuries, but most guys are too fucking insecure to admit it." She coughed a surprised giggle. "I'm not. When it comes to you and us, I'm gonna fuck up more often than I'd like."

She started to shake her head, but I held up a hand to stop her.

"It's because you make me irrational."

Her chin jerked back, and her tears were completely gone. I was halfway there. "You're one of the most clever-minded, rational people I know."

"In business," I agreed. "With you, I lose all sense of everything but us."

She tilted her head, but I pushed on. "Look at my track record. You know it's true."

"Kline." She reached for me, but I started to pace just outside of her range, before turning to face her again and kneeling on the wood floor in front of her feet.

Her hands reached desperately for mine, and this time I didn't deny them.

"I don't want to hold you back."

"I know you don't," she cut in.

"You're brilliant, and you deserve every facet of success you can get your hands on."

"Baby," she whispered.

I smiled and reached out to brush some stray hair from her

face, pulling her other hand flat to the pounding beat in my chest. My voice dropped to an intimate whisper as I admitted, "But I thought I was going to be along for the ride. I thought your success would flourish with me. At my company." I shrugged and finished with the part that bothered me most. "That I'd get to watch."

"Oh, Kline." She pulled my palm to her lips and kissed it.

"I'm so fucking proud of you. You're not where you are out of luck or chance. You're there because you deserve it. You're tenacious and smart, and God, I'd gotten used to sitting in on shit just so I could see it."

"I've been gone for months now, though," she pointed out gently. "If that's really it, why is it just bothering you now?"

I shrugged. "We're on our honeymoon. Thousands of miles away, just you and me. I know the traveling is coming, and baby, I'm going to miss you, but I'm prepared for it. Really."

Her brow creased in confusion.

"But I was fully expecting this to be *our* time. The calm before the storm. You, me, and absolutely nothing else. But it hasn't been that way. It's been you, me, and Wes, and I don't find him nearly as fucking pretty."

She laughed a little, a barely there smile of realization lifting the unbearable weight from her tiny shoulders.

"I feel a little like your aging wife, and your new job feels like your mistress. Unfortunately, it turns out I'm not above showing up naked in a trench coat in an effort to restore your interest."

"You're no aging wife. You run your own multibillion-dollar corporation, for God's sake."

"Not here, I don't. Here, I am nothing but your new husband. And I've selfishly been wishing you were here as only my wife."

"Couldn't this just be an opportunity to *watch me*?" she ventured, and I smiled.

"Ben."

"Ack. Okay. So you're right. I probably shouldn't be doing anything while I'm here."

"Me," I corrected playfully. "You should be doing nothing but me."

"Right, right. Don't worry, I've got you marked down on my to-do list."

"Thank God," I said with a wink.

"I'll call Wes and see if he can spare me for the rest of our time here," she offered.

"Oh, please, let me do it," I said a little too gleefully.

"No. Come on. He's your friend, but he's my boss. At least let me maintain a modicum of professionalism."

"I think that ship sailed, sweetheart. Back around Sexually-Influenced-Email-Island," I teased.

She flushed and slapped superficially at my chest. "That was your fault too!"

I smiled and waggled my eyebrows in triumph. She tried to resist, but in the end, she couldn't contain her smile either.

"Kline!"

"He's your boss, but trust me, this isn't Wes, your boss. This is Wes, my friend, and he's sitting back in New York merrily watching as he fucks with me. Let me call him."

"*Kline.*"

"That means yes. That's the same way you say my name during sex, and I *know* that means yes."

I grabbed her phone from the bed and scrolled through the numbers until I found Wes's office. She struggled to reach, but even on the tips of her toes, my outstretched arm kept her a good foot out of range of my ear.

It rang twice before his assistant answered. "Wes Lancaster's office."

I raised my voice an octave and did my best impression of my wife. "Hey, Gail, it's Georgia. Can you put me through?"

"Kline Brooks!" Georgia shrieked in the background.

I laughed and jogged out of the bedroom and onto the terrace, shutting the all-glass door behind me and holding it closed. My little Benny waved frantically on the other side.

"Georgia?" Gail questioned. She had to have been going through some fucking head trip. I didn't *sound* like Georgia, but it was sure as shit her number on the caller ID.

"That's me," I responded.

"Oh. Okay. I'll put you through," Gail muttered, mystified. I winked at Georgia through the glass and her eyes narrowed.

"Thanks!"

Wes's voice came over the line less than five seconds later. "Georgia?"

"Close," I said in my normal voice.

"Kline. Hey, buddy. How's the honeymoon?"

"Fucking fantastic," I said, telling him the truth but making sure my words had a little extra bite.

"Good, good," he murmured in response.

"Look. I know my wife is fucking essential to your operation," I started, diving right into the heart of it and turning to face the ocean so Georgia couldn't read my lips.

"Kline—"

"I handed her over on a silver fucking platter, so I know." He sighed, and I heard the door burst open behind me.

I kept talking anyway. "I don't know if you really needed her or if you just wanted to mess with me, but she's officially off duty for the rest of our trip."

"Yeah, I get it," he agreed, "and it was both. Messing with you and needing her."

I closed my eyes and forced myself to make an offer I really didn't want to extend. "You need to talk to her before you cut off all communication?"

"Yes!" Georgia demanded behind me. "Give me the phone."

"Yeah," Wes replied. "But it's not for work shit. I owe you, and I have a strong feeling you're in hot water."

I laughed. "Does your *feeling* have anything to do with the fact that you can hear my wife in the background?"

"It might," he said through a chuckle.

"Fine. Fix this, and we're even."

"Done."

Done. Because that was how problems between men got resolved.

Well, it was either that or hit each other in the face, and right now, neither of us was interested in making the trip.

CHAPTER 11

New York, Monday April 24th, Early Afternoon

Thatch

"He's been missing for four nights," Cassie said in my ear through the phone. Unable to avoid the office for more than a day, I'd given her my work number in case of an emergency or breakthrough. Apparently, she took those parameters very lightly. This was her tenth call today.

Yeah, I hear you. Yet again, I am the one answering her calls. Therefore, I'm still the idiot here.

"I know, honey. But I'm sure he's fine. He's scrappy. A real street cat. His assholishness might actually be coming in handy."

I'd gotten in touch with Kline's dad, and ever efficient, Bob had the vet on the hunt. But four long nights without an actual capture, and even I was starting to miss the little bastard. Or maybe I wasn't, but I was visualizing the pain in sweet Georgie's eyes when she heard the news and listening to near hysteria from her best friend at that very moment. Their pain was feeling very much like my pain.

"You think he's falling in line with the right cats, though?" she asked ridiculously. "Georgie'll be so pissed if she comes home to find him in a gang of runaways."

I rubbed at the tension in my forehead and turned my chair to face the floor-to-ceiling windows in my office.

"Well, if he does, we'll be here to force him into rehabilitation through intervention."

"Right," she scoffed, like *I* was the crazy one. "Like there's a cat rehab. Good one, Thatcher. It must be right next door to the cat detective."

"Cass—"

"I lied to her."

"Who? The cat detective?" I asked, completely lost.

"Wheorgie, numbnuts! I told her about the microchip, but I didn't tell her that we hadn't *actually* found him."

"The vet's been getting a signal," I told her, even though she already knew. I hoped that hearing it again might help to calm her down. "He's just been moving around too much to pinpoint an exact location for pickup."

"Yeah, Thatcher. I know all these things. Jesus."

Closing my eyes, I leaned back into my leather desk chair and sighed. "You called me. What exactly are you after here? Honest to God, I'm trying." *Harder than I would with anyone else*, I thought to myself. "But I can't for the life of me figure out what you want."

"I don't know either," she said, but fuck, the uncertainty, the longing—all of it made her simple words sound an awful lot like, *I just wanted to talk to you*.

"Cass—"

"I gotta go, T-bag. Let me know if you hear anything about Walnuts," she rushed out. And then with a quick click of the line, she was gone.

I spun around to my desk and tossed the phone in the cradle before rubbing a hand down my face in annoyance. Everything between us felt foreign, like I couldn't get a handle on it. The weirdest part was not knowing if I wanted to.

"Mr. Kelly?" my assistant, Madeline, called on the intercom. Reaching forward, I pushed the button on my phone panel to answer.

"Yeah?"

"There's someone on the line for you from Green Gardens in Frogsneck, NY?"

Fuck. That was the venue for my parent's surprise fortieth anniversary party next month. "Put them through, Mad."

"You got it."

Two quick rings confirmed her response before I put the phone to my ear. "Hey, Tom," I greeted. My hometown was the size of a chicken nugget, and only one person would be calling me from Green Gardens.

"Thatcher? It's Tom."

"Yeah, Tom. I got that. That's why I said 'Hey, Tom.'"

"Oh."

"The reason you're calling?" I prompted when silence consumed the line for nearly half a minute. It was times like these that made me really *not* miss home.

"Oh. Yeah. I know you said you wanted an open bar and that you wanted lobster *and* steak, but that's gonna be pretty expensive, bud. I just wanted to double-check before I made the order because once it's in, it's in. I can't do you any favors, even if I like you."

"Thanks, Tom, but I'm good. Open bar, lobster, *and* steak. Don't worry about the order, I won't leave you hanging."

"Oh, right, right," Tom agreed, taking a tone I knew well and absolutely hated. "I guess I forgot you're some hot shot zillionaire whoseewhatsit in the city these days."

My patience was unraveling, but I fought hard to pretend like I had some. "Yeah, that's not it, Tom. It's just my parents' fortieth. They deserve a nice night."

Mad gave a quick knock and peeked her red head in the door. "Someone is here for you," she mouthed.

I nodded and rushed to get Tom off the phone. "Listen, I have to go. But thanks for checking in. I really appreciate it."

"All right. I guess I'll put the order in if you're sure."

Mad peeked in again and raised her brows in question. Waving a big hand, I signaled to let whomever it was in.

"I'm sure. Thanks, Tom."

My eyebrows pulled together as Cassie bounded into my office while Mad held the door. She wore tight jeans and a crop top, and I'll admit, my gaze traveled to the bottom of her shirt—or half of a shirt—in the hopes there was boob swell to be seen more than once.

"You bet. I guess this means you'll be coming home soon, huh?" Tom asked, fucking refusing to get off the fucking phone. And with my new guest, I was obviously getting zero work done today.

"Yep," I said grudgingly. "That's what it means."

"How long's it been?"

Five years. It'd been five years.

"A few years," I murmured as I tried to make out Cassie's charades. Her arms waved and her tits bounced, and she'd just started to get down on the ground and crawl around on all fours.

Is she licking the tops of her hands and purring?

"Gotta go, Tom," I reiterated. "Thanks for checking in. See you soon."

The phone barely met its base before Cassie jumped to her feet. "Thank fuck. I thought you'd never get off the phone."

"What are you doing here, Cass? How the fuck did you know where my office was? And what in the *fuck* are you doing crawling around on my floor?"

"Well, hello to you too," she said, and it struck me like lightning. We were so similar, so like-minded. So much so, neither of us knew how to handle it. "And it's called Google, Thatcher."

"What's going on?" I asked again. "I thought you had somewhere to be. And how in the hell did you get here so fast? Do you have a teleportation device I need to try out?"

"Bob called me. Said he couldn't get through to you. The vet's got Walnuts." Her eyes fucking gleamed.

"Bob called when? Weren't you just crying to me about that little shit being missing?"

She shrugged. "Yeah, but that was just for fun. I was already on my way here."

"That was an act? An exercise in annoying me?" I asked.

She nodded and smiled.

"You're scary."

Her eyebrows just bounced.

"Well, shit. At least they found him." Air filled my lungs at the relief that I wouldn't have to tell Kline I'd permanently lost his wife's cat. "Thank fuck, right? You look relieved, and I'm sure Georgie will be too."

"Yep," she agreed with a bounce. "Thrilled all around." Too much bounce.

"What am I missing?"

"Let's just say Kline Brooks is going to have fucking hemorrhoids from trying to shit this load of news."

"*Fuck*."

CHAPTER 12

Cassie

"240 East 80th, please," I instructed the cabbie as Thatch slid in to sit beside me.

The cab driver was midforties, sloppily dressed, and sported a serious fucking scowl. I glanced at his driver's license on the dashboard and saw that Jenk was his name. I'd say it was apparent Ol' Jenkie boy was having a shit day.

"240 East 80th?" He glimpsed at us in the rearview mirror and then huffed out a sigh, death-gripping his steering wheel.

"Yes, please," I responded, trying to be sweet even though I felt like telling him to cool it on the attitude.

"Isn't that a friggin' vet hospital?" he snapped for some unknown reason. I honestly had no idea why driving us to a vet hospital would put him over the edge, but I did know that Jenk the fuckface wasn't just having a shit day, it was more like a shit year...or *life*.

"Well, shit. Who needs Google Maps when the world has men like you running around?" I retorted loud enough for him to hear. I *wanted* him to hear. Hell, he needed to hear it. This dude needed a reality check.

Thatch bumped me with his elbow, hoping I'd get the message and shut up. I turned to him and kept going. "Last time I checked, Jenk the fuckface was the cab driver. Not me or you. Sorry if we're not going to the destination of his liking, but them's the breaks when your job is to drive people around."

"What was that?" Jenk asked, beaming me with the stink-eye in the rearview mirror.

"I *said*—"

Thatch placed his hand over my mouth. "She said, she loves your hat. Go Mavericks!"

That wasn't even close to the content or length of what I'd said, but the cabbie nodded anyway, trying his hand at a stiff smile. It looked like a grimace, but I guess that was what happened to your face when you never smiled.

News flash, kids. Apparently, it will freeze that way.

"Our boys are lookin' good. I think we're gonna have one helluva season this year."

"That's not what I said, asshat," I muttered to Thatch.

"First rule of Fight Club, Cass. Don't start shit with the man behind the wheel. Especially when you're in *his* car and at his mercy."

"Whatever, Thatcher," I huffed out, adjusting myself in the leather seat and accidentally brushing my boob against Thatch's bicep in the process. Honestly, it was an accident. The Jolly Green Giant was practically taking up the whole back seat.

He sighed in response, shutting his eyes and holding the bridge of his nose with his forefinger and thumb. "Tell me your tits are out again. *Please.* I'm at the end of my rope here, but your tits have the ability to make all kinds of things grow."

I glanced down at my chest. *Shit.* "Uh, it's a really thin bra."

Yeah, I didn't have a bra on, and the air conditioning blasting in the cab had my nipples at full attention. It wasn't even on purpose. I'd been in the shower when Bob had called, and the second he told me the vet found Walter, I hauled ass to Thatch's office.

"Is it made out of fucking air?" he asked, voice hopeful and irritated at once. It seemed Thatcher was losing patience with the whole Walter, Cassie, and Thatch circus.

"What the fuck does it matter to you?" I snapped back. "If I want to walk around without a bra, that's my business, dude."

"Trust me, it's everyone's business when they have the power to save humanity from my mental breakdown."

"My nipples do not talk, and they don't have the power to save lives."

He glanced at me out of the corner of his eye. "Honey, they do. All they're doing right now is waving hello, and I already feel a million times better than I did five minutes ago. I bet Jenk feels better too."

Jenk didn't respond. And frankly, I took offense to that. Thatch noticed the change in me and pulled my attention back to him.

"Actually, right now, your tits are doing a 'we're stuck on a desert island and trying to wave down a plane,' kind of wave. Not just a hello. That means their power is double."

The ridiculousness of this entire conversation had me laughing. "Fuck, for a numbers guy, you're imaginative. I'll give you that."

He smirked. "Your tits put all sorts of creative ideas in my head, honey."

I eye-fucked him for a good ten seconds, honing in on the crotch of his dress slacks before meeting his eyes. "Put your boner away, Thatcher."

He glanced at my tits and then his dark brown eyes held my gaze as he nodded toward them. "Do it for me, Cassie."

We were at a stalemate, just staring at one another, the "let's fuck" tension building with each second, and I wasn't sure if it would end with me smacking the shit out of him or getting his dick out. Hell, maybe both.

The cab's brakes squealed as we came to an abrupt stop, and my face almost hit the back of the driver's seat.

"We're here!" Jenk shouted over his shoulder. "Fifteen bucks and I don't got fucking change."

While Thatch pulled his wallet out of his back pocket and tossed money into the front seat, I hopped out and turned toward the open window on the driver's side, ready to give the cabbie a piece of my mind.

"Wow, you really fucking suck at—" I started to say, but strong arms wrapped around my middle and carried me toward the entrance of the animal hospital.

"Fuck you hard, Thatcher! That guy needs to know he's a fucking *asshole*!" I shouted loud enough for most of Manhattan to hear.

Thatch just laughed in my ear while carrying me toward the doors. Each chuckle fueled my fake rage.

"The second you set me down, I'd protect my balls if I were you."

His lips were near my ear. "I'd love to wrestle you, maybe wind up tangled in your deliciously free tits, but we're about to go in to get Walter, and if you're acting like a lunatic, they probably won't let us take him home. And if we don't get that little asshole home, then you'll be the one who has to break that news to Georgia."

He was so strong and gentle at the same time, and he didn't seem anything but amused by my antics. I ignored the mating call from my puss-ay. If it were up to her, I'd have Thatch'd that in the cab. "*Fine.* Just set me down, motherfucker."

He set me down, and I strode into the office, not wasting any time holding the door for him.

"We've tried to separate them, but Walter isn't really having it," the vet tech stated vaguely, guiding us toward the back room where cages were lined up and stacked on top of one another.

"What do you mean 'Walter isn't really having it'?" Thatch asked, sliding his hands into his pockets as we stood in front of a cage holding one big motherfucker of a dog.

"Well…" She trailed off hesitantly. "He just gets really upset."

I put a hand on my hip. "Upset? You're going to have to explain what Walter getting upset looks like. That cat generally shows two emotions—utter indifference or satisfaction from spending three hours licking his asshole."

Thatch nodded. "Yeah, he's pretty big on the asshole licking. Is that normal?"

"Um, yes. Actually, that's very normal," she responded as she opened a drawer by the dog's cage. "Cats are predators. Their instincts are to clean themselves to avoid being scented by their prey."

Thatch smirked at me while Julie, the vet tech, was busy rummaging through a drawer full of collars and leashes. "Maybe we should start licking your tits to see if it'd help deter horny motherfuckers from staring," he whispered.

I cocked an eyebrow. "*We?*"

He shrugged. "Figured you'd need help. Most chicks can't get their tongues to their nipples without pulling a muscle in the process."

"That's very generous of you, but there's no risk of injury when it comes to sucking on my own tits."

His eyes heated, and he stepped closer. "Prove. It."

I grinned. "Make. Me."

"Here it is!" Julie yelled victoriously, waving a collar and leash in the air.

"This conversation isn't over, honey," Thatch muttered.

"Meh, I'm already over it," I retorted before turning my attention to Julie. "That collar looks a little small for that dog." I nodded toward the cage she was in the process of unlatching.

"It's not for him, it's for Walter," Julie said with a laugh. Before she unhooked the final latch, she stopped abruptly. "I almost forgot the gloves!" she said, grabbing an oversized pair from the counter beside her.

"Gloves?" Thatch questioned, eyebrows raised.

"When Walter gets upset, he tends to scratch a lot."

"Okay…but why are you opening that dog's cage? You know Walter is a cat, right?"

I glanced at Thatch, and it was apparent I wasn't the only one confused.

"Walter is inside this cage," she answered.

"What?" we said at the same time.

Julie nodded and opened the cage door. She nudged the giant dog to the side, and sure enough, there was the little dickhead, curled up against the dog's back.

"This is Walter's new friend?" I asked, eyes wide and shocked.

When Bob had called, he'd said the vet had warned him that The Asshole had a new friend he wasn't too keen on being removed from. I had assumed it was a cat, a female cat, but apparently my assumptions about Georgia's little buddy were dead wrong. And judging by the size of the balls on the dog he was curled up to, this little dickhead was on Team Dean.

"Yep," Julie announced on a whisper as she attempted to pick up Walnuts carefully without waking him. "Walter has really taken a liking to Stan here."

I glanced at Thatch and knew the second he got an eyeful of Stan's gonads.

"Seems there's a bigger reason behind Walter's enjoyment of

tossing his own salad."

I snorted in laughter, and Julie just glanced over her shoulder, confusion stamped on her face.

This poor girl. She was so sweet, and yet somehow, she'd managed to pull the short straw and get stuck with Thatch and me. Two assholes who had no filters.

And all at once, it hit me.

Thatch and I were very alike. Almost *too* alike.

I stared at him, taking in his stupid, sexy smirk. *Jesus.* He was the guy version of me.

"You okay, honey?" he asked, his gaze catching on the befuddled expression gracing my face.

"Yep," I answered, averting my eyes and trying like hell to forget that revelation.

But I couldn't.

If opposites attracted, then what in the hell was happening between numbnuts and me?

An ear-piercing shriek grabbed my attention.

"It's okay, Walter," Julie cooed as she tried to disentangle his paws from the cage.

Was he fucking holding on to the cage door?

More shrieking and clawing echoed inside the large room. Other pets started to take notice, standing up in their cages and watching shit hit the fan before their curious eyes.

Stan woke up from his slumber and started barking like a banshee. And within minutes, the entire room was filled with barking and growling and cages rattling.

"Holy fucking shit!" I covered my ears.

"This looks like a bit of a problem, Julie," Thatch shouted over the rising noise.

She just nodded, sweat dripping from her forehead, and resumed wrestling with Walter, who now had the support of his boyfriend. Stan's teeth were wrapped around the leash connected to Walter's collar, and he was tugging the cat back into the cage.

"Hey, Julie, you guys wouldn't happen to offer pet boarding services would you?" Thatch's voice boomed over the barks.

"Yes, sir, we do!"

"Fantastic!" He clapped his hands together. "Let's go ahead and let Walter spend more time with Ol' Stan here, and I'll just cover boarding until my buddy and his wife get back from their honeymoon."

I actually heard her sigh of relief over the barks.

"It's weird. All we've really talked about are my tits and his boner, but there's a strange connection there," I told Georgia over the phone, fiddling with a napkin on the bistro table.

I called her to fess up about my lie of omission and let her know that Walnuts would be staying with his boyfriend until they got back from their honeymoon. I just chose to start the conversation off on a much lighter note. And for some reason, the weirdness between me and Thatch seemed like the best lead-in.

"That's *all* you've talked about?" she asked, shock in her voice.

My eyes caught sight of Thatch standing at the coffee shop counter, ordering our drinks and food. After the shit show at the vet's office, we decided to grab a bite about ten blocks away from my apartment. Well, *I* decided, and he bitched about the distance from his office, but he still came along regardless.

Why we were doing this was a mystery, but here we were.

"Pretty much," I answered. It was the truth. His boner and my tits seemed to be the number one topic of discussion whenever we were together. Yet another mystery that needed to be solved.

"For the love of God, why?"

I shrugged. "Mostly because they're out, I guess. My tits and his boner."

"Jesus. Next time you're around him, make like an evangelical and cover those things up. See if that helps…" She paused, and then added, "*Wait… What do you mean they're out?*"

Thatch smirked at the barista, and her cheeks flushed pink. For fuck's sake, he held some kind of magical power over women. One smile and he had the girl making our coffee two seconds away from convulsing into a spontaneous orgasm.

What would he be like in bed?

My mind took that as a green light to conjure up the possibilities—me riding his face, him fucking me with my legs in the air, my tongue sliding up his shaft, my tits wrapped around his cock… Yeah, they were some wickedly dirty fantasies.

My brain and pussy were convinced he'd be a fantastic fuck, and that only made me more intrigued about Thatcher Kelly.

"Cass? Are you still there?" Georgia's voice filled my ear.

"Yep."

"You totally just drifted off into 'I'm gonna Thatch that' fantasyland."

"Yep," I agreed.

"Just promise me you'll wait to screw his brains out until after you leave the restaurant. I'd like to enjoy the rest of my honeymoon without trying to wire you bail money."

"I'm not gonna fuck Thatch," I lied.

Wait…what? Was I already planning on getting in the Jolly Green Giant's pants?

I'd save that question to mull over at a later time. Preferably when he wasn't heading toward me with his arms full of coffee and blueberry muffins.

She snorted in laughter. "Yeah, and I'm not looking forward to riding my husband's cock in about five minutes."

"He's standing there with his giant schlong in front of your face, isn't he?"

Georgia giggled.

"All right, well, before you have your mouthful of pee-nis, I need to give you the rundown on Walnuts."

"Okay," she muttered, already sounding distracted.

Perfect.

I took a deep breath and said everything in a rush. "We actually just found him a few hours ago. He's good. Sorry I lied. He's at the vet. Gonna stay there until you guys get back because I've got a shoot, and obviously, we're really bad babysitters. So it's better that way. Okayloveyoubye."

I hit end on the call as Thatch sat across from me at the table, setting my coffee and muffin before me.

"She take it well?" he asked, his long fingers sliding the wrapper off his muffin with surprising finesse.

Yeah, he could definitely butter my muffin. Any fucking day of the week.

"I don't know." I shrugged.

Thatch chuckled. "You hung up before she even responded, didn't you?"

"Yep," I answered, taking a sip from my coffee. "You use that same tactic with Kline, don't you?"

He nodded. "All the fucking time."

Man, we were so much alike it was creepy.

My phone vibrated across the table with a text notification.

Georgia: You're lucky I'm in a different time zone. Text me the vet's info.

Me: You're a surprisingly good multitasker.

Georgia: Why are we friends?

Me: Less typing. More sucking. P.S. Friends don't let friends blow and text at the same time, Wheorgie. It's dangerous.

Georgia: Put a bra on.

I laughed out loud at that one.

Thatch tilted his head to the side. "What's so funny?"

I held my phone out to him, letting him see the conversation. He chuckled a few times and then took it upon himself to snatch my phone and start scrolling through my shit.

"Oh, so it's like that, is it?" I held out my hand. "If you want to be nosy, it has to be on equal terms."

He didn't bat an eye at my demand, sliding his phone out of his pocket and across the table.

To be honest, I was a little surprised by his openness, but I probably shouldn't have been. I didn't have anything to hide or be embarrassed about. Therefore, the guy version of me probably didn't either.

Shit. The asshat didn't even have a passcode set up on his phone.

My fingers tapped on his pictures first, scrolling through numerous photos of sports games and hilarious candids of his friends. I stopped on one that made me smile. "Are you wearing a 'Single and Ready to Mingle' shirt in this pic?"

"Fuck yeah, I am. Don't knock the shirt, it's my favorite."

"I'm stealing that shirt. I'll fucking wrestle you for it if I have to."

"You don't need to come up with excuses to wrestle me, honey. Name the time and place and lose the crop top, and I'm there."

I laughed. "Keep dreaming."

"All dreams can come true, if we have the courage to pursue

them."

"Did you just quote Walt Disney in the context of getting me naked?"

"Sure did," he said, eyes back on my phone.

I moved to his contacts next, finding a slew of female names.

"Who's Tasara?" I asked, clicking on her name and finding a picture of an extremely attractive brunette.

His eyes met mine. "Who's Sean?"

"My brother," I answered honestly.

"Your brother? You know he's black, right?"

My eyes narrowed, and I flipped him the bird. He just smirked.

"Tell me about Tasara," I demanded. "And do you make a point of taking pictures of all of your contacts?"

"Tasara is my sister, and yes, I do. It's one of my favorite things."

"She is not your sister," I said, laughing.

"Nah, but she's a really nice girl."

"How nice?" I asked, wanting some details. I was curious about this man and the way he handled relationships.

"She's a fucking *giver.*"

I tapped another name and stumbled upon yet another picture of a different gorgeous face. "What about Rachel?"

"She's a sweetheart. A really down-to-earth cool chick."

Next contact. "And Samantha?"

"She's a doll. Definitely a bit wild."

"You don't like wild?" I asked.

He smirked and raised his eyebrows, sitting back in his chair. "I *love* wild."

Of course he did.

"What about JoAnna?"

"She's a *multiples* kind of girl."

"And Ella, is she a wild sweetheart too?"

"All of those girls are sweethearts," he corrected. "I don't waste my time on anything else. But Ella did have a bit of a wild streak, too. I tend to migrate toward that kind of woman," he answered with a knowing glance.

My chest stung—like an actual stinging, burning feeling—and I found my hand rubbing it seeking relief. So many girls, but he didn't even hesitate to put details to a name. They weren't all faceless screws; that was apparent.

Was I having a heart attack?

This was definitely something I had never felt before. Fuck, I hated it. I knew that much. And the more I scrolled, the worse the pain got. I looked away from the screen, wanting a reprieve from the torturous feeling, or whatever the hell it was.

I guess if I keeled over while stuffing my face, I'd know the root cause was clogged arteries.

"So, these girls, how does it work? Are they actually cool with the fact that you're not a one-chick kind of guy? Or is that something you don't tell them?" I asked, no disdain in my voice. I was honestly just curious.

"Of course, they know the score, honey. I've been open and honest with every woman I've ever been with. I don't feed women bullshit lies to get in their pants. Never have and never will." He set my phone on the table. "And who said I wasn't a monogamous kind of guy?"

I cocked an eyebrow, sliding his phone toward him. Trapping the phone to a stop, his big hand spanned nearly the entire tiny table. "No one said it. I just assumed you're more focused on playing the field than actually looking for The One."

A hard-to-decipher emotion crossed his face, but I knew it wasn't happiness. There was some sort of sadness lying beneath the surface of his brown eyes.

"I'm not judging, Thatch. Honestly. I'm not exactly known for settling down, either."

He spun his phone on the table and glanced up at me. "Do you think you ever will?"

I shrugged. "I'm not sure. I guess if I found the right person, I would. What about you?"

"Same. I don't have my future mapped out, but I'm always open to possibilities."

I glanced at the time on my phone and realize I only had about an hour to get home, pack, and get to the airport. "Shit, I better get out of here," I announced, standing up from my chair.

Thatch glanced around, confused. "You have somewhere to be?"

I picked my purse up off the ground, sliding it over my shoulder. "Yeah, I've got a flight to catch."

"A flight?" He stood up, grabbing our empty cups and discarded wrappers, and tossed them in the trash can across from our table.

"A few last-minute shoots in the Bahamas. Just found out this morning."

He looked surprised. "You're flying to the Bahamas? *Today?* For a photo shoot?"

"Yeah, ESPN asked me to do a couple of pictorials… I'm pretty sure I'm speaking English right now…"

He ignored my sarcastic retort. "Why didn't you say anything about it?"

"It just slipped my mind," I said, walking beside him as we headed out of the coffee shop.

He held open the door. "How long are you going to be gone?"

"Not sure. Three, maybe four, weeks tops."

Thatch stopped abruptly in the middle of the sidewalk. "You're going to be gone an entire month?"

My face scrunched up in confusion. "Yeah, is that okay?"

He ran a hand through his hair. "I guess so, yeah."

"Is your boner going to miss me, Thatcher?" I teased.

He chuckled, but he stepped closer to me. "Your tits? Fuck yes. You? Eh, I think I'll be okay. Maybe I'll even manage to get some work done without you calling my office fifteen times a day."

I grinned, standing on my tiptoes to kiss his cheek. "Don't worry, T-bag, I'll set time aside out of my busy schedule to brighten your day with my beautiful voice."

He smiled back, eyes amused. "At the very least, shoot me a text so I know you made it there safely."

"You got it," I agreed. "Bye, Thatch," I said, turning and heading for my apartment.

A smack to my ass startled a squeal from my lips and stopped my feet dead in their tracks. I turned back around to find him smirking and walking backward in the opposite direction.

"Be good, Cass!"

"I don't know about that, Thatcher! I'm feelin' a bit *wild*!"

"Be. Good," he demanded and then turned on his heels, getting lost in the crowd.

Be good?

What in the fuck did that even mean? And more importantly, why did I care?

He didn't have a say in what I did or didn't do. But fuck, he sure had a say in whether or not he wiggled his way into my head. Like a leech, he had taken up residence in my thoughts, and I wasn't sure how to get rid of him.

Did I even want to?

CHAPTER 13

New York, Monday, May 1st, Late Afternoon

Georgia

I was damn near bouncing in the car as Frank drove us to the vet's office to pick up Walter. In the two weeks since I'd seen him, he'd been forced to spend time with Cassie and Thatch *and* gone missing. I could hardly fathom the thought of him roaming the city streets by himself, but bearing Cassie's disdain probably wasn't much better.

"Little excited, Benny?" Kline asked, placing a soothing hand on my thigh to stop my leg from bouncing.

I held out my thumb and forefinger, adding, "Just a little bit."

He grinned, wrapping his arm around my shoulders and tucking me close to his side.

Instead of going home and catching some shut-eye after a long flight, I had convinced Kline to go straight from the airport to pick up my little buddy. Well, maybe less *convinced*, more told him if he didn't go, I still was. Walter didn't need to stay another night in a cold crate. He needed to be home with his family.

Kline kissed my forehead. "Thanks for a wonderful honeymoon, Mrs. Brooks."

I looked up at him, my heart in my eyes. "Likewise, Mr. Brooks. I'll probably be bow-legged for the next three months, but I had the best time. You're real good at honeymoons."

He smirked, tucking a lone curl behind my ear. "Who says that treatment stops after the honeymoon? Consider yourself thoroughly well-fucked and bow-legged for the next hundred years."

I laughed, grinning back at him. "If you can still fuck me like that when we're ninety years old, you're not real."

"Should I expect a blood test? A surgical examination?"

"Gross."

One perfect eye shut in a wink. "I'm real, Benny. *Really* in fucking love with my wife, and love has the power to do crazy things. I'm just hopeful those things include giving a ninety-year-old man the stamina to keep his pretty little wife *satisfied*."

"Jesus. Cool it on the swoon, you bastard. I might actually pass out from it."

He didn't cool it, though—his blue eyes still smoldered.

"Kline!" I smacked his chest. "I'm being serious."

"No, you're not." He leaned in close, whispering in my ear, "You love the swoon. In fact, you're already thinking about how to get me naked the second we get home."

"Shut up," I said through a giggle. He wasn't too far off base with that one though. My mind was considering the backseat of the car, but I'd keep that to myself.

He laughed and placed a soft kiss on my lips. "You won't have to try very hard." His nose rubbed mine and his voice dropped to a whisper. "With me, you'll never even have to ask."

Like I said, swoony motherfucking bastard.

God, I loved him.

I should've known things weren't going to go smoothly the minute we stepped into the vet's office. Few words were spoken in exchange with the receptionist, but as soon as we mentioned we were there to pick up Walter, utter panic consumed her face. She muttered something about getting Julie and then strode off without another word. *A bad omen.*

Fifteen minutes and a brief video on veterinarian-office safety later, we were standing in front of the crate of a Great Dane named Stan. *I knew that video wasn't standard procedure.*

"We're actually here to pick up Walter," Kline instructed. "Walter is a cat."

Julie pointed to the cage. "Yeah, well, Walter is actually inside there."

We looked at one another, confused.

"What do you mean he's in there?" I asked.

"He's really taken a liking to Stan and quite adamantly refuses to be anywhere but curled up next to Stan's back."

"He's taken a liking to this giant dog? This giant, *male dog?*" Kline questioned, eyes wide.

"Honestly, I've never seen anything like it," Julie admitted. "They seem very attached to one another."

"*Christ.*" Kline ran his hand through his hair, visibly disturbed by the whole scenario.

I leaned toward the cage, peering inside until I saw the fluff of multicolored dark and light fur that was Walter. "Holy moly, he's really in there."

"Yes, he really is," Julie said, exasperated.

"Well, let's get him out so we can take him home." It was obvious Kline was ready to get home and relax. Being on a plane for over thirteen hours tended to do that to a person.

"That's actually easier said than done, Mr. Brooks," Julie replied, turning to look at both of us. "Your friends didn't tell you what happened when they tried to pick him up?"

"No." I shook my head. I had a feeling Cassie left out the important details for a reason—like making sure we suffered through this without warning.

"What exactly happened?" Kline asked, tone hinting at irritation.

Thatch would definitely be getting an earful later. Kline Brooks wasn't the kind of guy you sent in blind. The fallout would probably be entertaining to watch, though.

"Walter gets very…intense whenever we try to remove him from Stan's cage."

"Intense?" My eyes nearly bugged out of my head.

Julie nodded. "*Violently* intense."

This doesn't sound good.

"With all due respect, Julie, my wife and I have been on a plane all day. I'd really like to just get Walter and head on home, so what exactly do we need to do to make that happen?"

"I'll get suited up, and we can give it another shot," she said, turning on her heels and striding through a door toward a back room.

"Suited up?" I asked, my concern growing by the minute.

Kline just sighed, shaking his head. "Fuck if I even know what that means, but I don't fucking like the sound of it."

Yeah, my husband was pretty much done with this entire scenario, and I had a feeling we hadn't even really seen anything yet. When he started throwing around f-bombs, I knew his ironclad patience was on its last legs.

Julie came out of the back room with a lot more clothing on than she started with. She looked like she had wrapped herself up in a mattress and thrown on some type of heavy-duty, protective clothing over top. Her hands were covered in giant gloves, and a hard hat adorned her head.

"You have *got* to be shitting me," Kline muttered to himself.

"Uh…Julie? You need that much…*gear*? Just to get our cat out of the cage?"

"Yes." She nodded, face determined. "You'll see."

You'll see? Talk about ominous. This just got worse and worse.

She stood in front of the cage and took a deep breath, mumbling something to herself. She looked like she was preparing to exchange gunfire with terrorists. Her hands shook as they unlatched the door and reached inside to nudge Stan off to the side.

I was starting to think this whole thing was a bit dramatic, but then, as she wrapped her gloves around Walter's body, I realized it wasn't dramatic at all. Not one bit. Hell, she probably should have worn more gear.

Walter screeched and clawed, banshee cries louder than I'd ever heard echoed through the room as he valiantly fought her efforts.

"It's okay, Walter," she cooed, but he wasn't having one bit of it. His claws dug into the padding on her arms, making any question of its necessity vanish.

My hand covered my mouth in shock, and Kline just muttered, "Oh, for fuck's sake."

"Come on, Walter, your mom and dad are here to pick you up," Julie soothed, trying her damnedest to comfort a cat who wanted no fucking comfort.

More screeching and clawing.

Was he holding on to the cage?

Stan woke up at that moment and started barking—loud, deep barks that filled the room and started to wake up the other dogs.

Within minutes, every animal was losing their shit.

Walter's paws lost their grip on the cage, but somehow, he managed to latch himself onto Stan, holding on to him for dear life. Stan's eyes found his, and they weren't the angry eyes of a clawed dog, but those of a companion offering encouragement.

Oh. My. God. My buddy was in love!

That's why he didn't want to leave Stan. Tears filled my eyes as I watched Julie yank Walter out of the cage and slam the door shut. Stan stood on his legs, howling in distress. He'd found The One while Kline and I were on our honeymoon.

"We can't tear them apart, Kline!" I cried. "They're in love!"

Kline looked away from the sight of Julie wrestling Walter into a traveling crate, and his eyes met mine. His brow was scrunched, and he was staring at me like I had truly lost it.

"Kline, I'm being serious. They love each other. We can't tear them apart."

He scrubbed a hand over his face, muttering, "I'm going to fucking *kill* Thatch."

Julie managed to get Walter inside the traveling crate and lock the door, and all I could do was watch as my cat and his new boyfriend cried for each other. Stan howled. Walter screeched. It was the saddest fucking thing I'd ever seen.

"Can we take Stan home?" I asked Julie.

"No," my husband interjected. "Baby, I love you, I really do, but we are not taking that dog home with us."

"But Kline," I started to plead, but he wasn't having it.

He shook his head. "He's a Great Dane, Georgia. And he's not even full grown yet. He probably has another fifty pounds to go. There is no way in hell we can bring him back to the apartment."

Even though I knew he was right, I still wasn't happy. I knew our co-op only allowed pets under twenty-five pounds, but I couldn't stop myself from being irrationally angry with Kline for not letting us take Stan.

"We also have a two-week waiting period," Julie offered, trying to smooth things over. When my eyes jumped to hers, she explained. "To see if anyone claims him. He's a suspected lost pet too."

Kline's eyes were relieved. That made one of us.

"Fine," I cried, then grabbed Walter's crate, and stomped off toward the exit.

Kline followed quickly, but I turned to him just as we reached the door and pointed an irrational finger in his face. "You may not want a dog, but you're gonna be needing a fucking dog house."

Mic drop. Georgia out.

New York, Sunday, May 7ᵗʰ, Late Morning

We had been home for about a week since the vet debacle, and I'd managed to stop blaming Kline for the reason Stan wasn't at our apartment, but Walter was still sulking.

Actually, we were both sulking.

For the past six days, if I wasn't working, Walter and I were lying in bed, watching reruns of *Friends* together. He only seemed to perk up when the episode where Phoebe sings "Smelly Cat" was on. We had watched that episode, *The One With The Baby On The Bus*, a good fifteen times.

My husband did his best to cheer me up, but I still couldn't get over the fact that Walter's little kitty heart was breaking. It was his first true love, and it was playing out like an animal version of *Romeo and Juliet*. Well, without the families at war or the poison or the whole guy and girl scenario, but yeah, it was definitely a tragic, star-crossed love story.

When Julie had told us that the second Stan walked into the office, Walter had sidled up to the big dog and started cleaning his fur, I knew, without a doubt, it had been love at first lick.

My poor little buddy.

And now, I was going to have to leave him to mourn by himself.

Wes had asked me to join him on a recruiting trip for the Mavericks, and even though I'd much rather stay home and console my heartbroken cat than go to Phoenix for the next week, I needed to go. I needed to start getting my feet wet and diving headfirst into my job with the Mavericks' organization.

I tossed my toiletries into my suitcase and zipped it shut. Sitting on the bed beside Walter and stroking my fingers behind his ears, I said, "It'll be okay, buddy. I promise, it'll be okay."

He purred, but his eyes were still sad.

Kline walked into the bedroom, leaning against the doorframe. "All set?"

I nodded, stood up from the bed, and kissed the top of Walter's head. "I'll be back in a week, buddy. Be good for Kline while I'm gone."

My husband grabbed my suitcase, and I followed his lead into the hallway.

"Promise me you'll take good care of Walter while I'm gone," I said as we stepped into the elevator.

"I promise, baby."

"My kind of good care," I specified.

"Nothing but the best for the grumpy cat," he assured me.

"And promise me you'll take him places. He needs to get out of the apartment. I think it would be good for him while I'm gone."

He grinned, laughing and groaning softly. "I promise. You have nothing to worry about, sweetheart. Walter and I will bond like fucking hydrogen while you're gone."

I moved closer to him, wrapping my arms around his waist and looking up into his blue eyes. "What about you? Will my husband be okay, too?"

He pressed a soft kiss to my lips. "I'll be missing you for the next week, but there's only one thing I need to hear to make it okay."

I smiled. "I'll be missing you too."

CHAPTER 14

New Jersey/New York, Wednesday, May 10ᵗʰ, Late Morning

Kline

Sunlight streaked through the windshield as I pulled to a stop and put the rental car in park. I'd have to do something more permanent about our lack of vehicle eventually, but I wanted to leave *something* for when Georgie got home. There was a risk she'd be feeling left out or pushed at that point thanks to my unconventionally large surprises, and I wanted at least one thing to be completely of her making. Picking out a couple of cars seemed like a good start.

I'd seen fifteen houses in the last two days, and not one of them had been right. Too big or too small, I was starting to feel a little like Goldilocks—lost and tired and hoping someone would show up with some beds. But my Realtor said she had a feeling about this one, and it was located less than thirty minutes from Georgia's parents, Dick and Savannah, in a pretty little town in New Jersey. I wasn't sure if that was really a pro or a con, but thirty minutes was safe either way—far enough if she didn't want to be close, just a short trip if she did. And the work commute to the city wouldn't be traumatizing either. It often took more than thirty minutes to get from one place in the city to the other anyway.

"Well, what do you think?" I asked, turning to my only companion and helper in the search for the perfect home.

He didn't say much, but then, I didn't really expect him to. We were really just starting to come to terms with one another, and he still felt lingering animosity about our most recent disagreement. But Georgie trusted him, so I knew making an effort to show I did too would go a long way toward making her feel comfortable about our new normal. Even though she was the only one going through a major professional change, we were still very much a *we* now, and I wanted the change to get marked with just enough significance.

"I'm not sure yet either," I told Walter. "Maybe you'll know once you lick yourself in a few rooms."

He meowed in agreement, a huge step in the right direction, and then leaned his head toward me so I could hook the thin leash to his collar.

I hopped out first and helped him to the ground so he wouldn't hurt his paws. The picture of us together was ridiculous—confirmed by the Realtor's face on the first day. *Kline Brooks, the eccentric billionaire who goes nowhere without his cat.*

Far from the truth, but luckily, all I'd had to say was "my wife loves this cat" for the sweet, middle-aged woman to understand.

"Mr. Brooks," she greeted us as Walter and I climbed the small hill of the driveway.

"Hey, Helen," I replied, watching with never-ending fascination as she got down on her knees and greeted Walter with strokes and kisses.

"Hello, Walter," she cooed in his little kitty ear. I swear, this cat was *catnip* for women. But I guess most of them did love a good asshole.

Holding out a hand, I helped Helen to her feet, and we made

our way toward the front door. A huge front porch lined the entire front of the house, and a swing hung in the far right corner. Soft tan siding covered the guts, and tasteful black-and-white accents made up the trim, shutters, and door. So far, so good.

"From what you've told me, I think this one is really going to hit on all of Georgia's tastes. Simple, updated, but with a ton of character in the moldings and fixtures," Helen explained as she worked the lockbox to retrieve the key. "It's just gone on the market, and I think it's priced pretty fair, so there's a good chance it's going to move fast."

"And how much property?" I asked as I glanced down at Walter.

"Just over four acres. The backyard is large and well-maintained, but we'll get to that. I think it's got a lot of possibility if you're thinking about more pets." She smirked and shrugged. "Or maybe some kids?"

I just laughed, not about to discuss my family's future plans with Helen before discussing it with my wife, but I appreciated the woman's sentiment. She could tell I wanted to make a home for Georgie that had room for *all* the possibilities.

Nothing made me happier than making Benny happy, and Walter on a fucking leash beside me made that really fucking apparent.

"And you told the seller about the quick close?"

"Yes. They're completely on board. If you're interested and pay a premium," she said, cocking her head and smiling. Almost everyone got motivated when you paid extra. "They'll happily close by the end of this week. But, that does mean we really have to make a quick decision."

I hummed my agreement. I'd know by the end of the tour. Georgie had been laying down plenty of information about what she preferred and what she didn't while she helped me with my parents' Hamptons house, and I'd been storing it all up like a fucking library.

As we stepped through the front door, Walter took off and pulled the leash right out of my hand. Straight through the large, open space, he immediately settled in front of the wall-to-wall glass windows at the back and started licking himself. I took that to mean he liked it.

"Isn't that adorable?" Helen commented, putting a hand to her chest and sighing. Apparently, Walter knew how to lay on the swoon. I, personally, didn't fucking see it, but what did I know?

"So it's five bedrooms, open floor plan, as you can see. The kitchen is huge, maybe a little overdone for the rest of the house, but it's *beautiful*. Antique white cabinets and fresh quartz counters."

She spoke, and I listened as I walked, scanning the space and immediately picturing us living there. Everything reeked of Georgie, from the dark wood floors, to the serene blue-gray on the walls, and when the kitchen came into view, it hit me. She and me and little blue-eyed babies carefully perched on the edge of the counter. I could see spilled milk and lazy Sundays and more goddamn happiness than my chest could contain.

"The floor is—"

"This is it," I cut in, knowing I'd spend some of the best years of my life here.

"Don't you want to see the bedrooms? And the basement? And the backyard?" Helen asked rapid-fire.

"Sure," I said, because I knew I shouldn't buy a house I hadn't even seen in its entirety, but this was it. I knew it on a cellular level.

This. This was the home my wife would love and had never once asked for. All the things I'd ever hoped to find in a woman lived in her. When she looked at me, she didn't see anything other than love and her one true match—and maybe a big dick.

"Why don't you go ahead and call the seller while we walk the rest?"

"But what if you see something you don't like?" Helen asked.

With a gentle hand at her elbow, I tried to convey just how sure I was. "Helen, the only thing that's gonna stop me from buying this house is a body in the basement. And even then, I might overlook it if they can give me a good reason."

"Okay, Walt. You have to stay in the car for this one."

A hiss and swipe of his claw.

"I get it. I know you know where we are. I'm not really sure *how* you know because you're a cat, but I know you know."

He let loose with a suspicious, mewling meow.

"After the way things went when we picked you up, they've forbidden you to come back in there. But I promise, everyone is going to be really happy when I come back out." He seemed somewhat placated. "Well, probably everyone but me," I added, which turned his kitty expression into satisfaction.

"Right," I said to him and myself, and hoped that, one day, I'd either stop talking to my cat or stop feeling so ridiculous about it.

I shut the car door with a slam and walked up to the building, the bell over the door ringing as I stepped inside.

The receptionist looked up from her paperwork with a smile, ready to greet me, but when she saw who it was, the smile melted right off of her face.

"Walter's in the car. With the windows rolled down," I said, not wasting any time setting everyone's mind at ease. The tension in her shoulders relaxed immediately, answering the question of whether she had a neck or not affirmatively. "I called and talked to Julie, and she said there'd been no one looking to claim Stan."

Julie stepped through the door from the back. She smiled freely, but she'd had fair warning of my arrival—and the chance to remind me that Walter was strictly prohibited from entering the building.

"Hey, Mr. Brooks. Come on back. I'm pretty sure Stan is going to be happy to see you."

With a nod to Receptionist Melanie, I stepped through the door as Julie held it open. Barking filled my ears, but it wasn't Stan. The fucking enormous Great Dane puppy lay sleeping in the center of his cage, curled up into the tightest coil he could manage.

"All he's really been doing since you guys left is sleeping," Julie explained. "I think he's been depressed."

He did seem to frown in his sleep, and I was happy Georgie wasn't seeing him like this.

"I can open the cage for you," Julie offered, pulling my eyes to her. "He's really big, but super gentle. Walter seemed to be the violent one of the two."

That much I could believe.

I nodded my agreement, and she pulled up the latch and swung open the door.

"Hey, Stan," I whispered to warn him I was there. He opened his big black eyes just as I reached out to touch him, leaned into my hand, and blew out a big doggie breath. "You ready to come home?"

CHAPTER 15

Phoenix, Friday, May 12ᵗʰ, Very Late Night

Georgia

Five days away from Kline had been five too many. Phone calls, text messages, video chats, emails, none of them lived up to the real thing. Which was why I was sitting on a red-eye flight from Phoenix to New York. My work travel had only just begun, but I could already tell it'd never be the highlight of my job.

When I'd told Wes I wasn't flying home with the team, he had laughed at the hilarity of me missing my husband after only five days. Thankfully, he'd ended his laughter by being surprisingly supportive, even though he let me know how ridiculous he thought it was.

But I didn't care that I was sitting in a cramped coach seat versus the luxury leather recliners on the team's jet. I didn't care that I was dead on my feet and about one blink away from falling into a coma. I just wanted to get home to my husband.

I slid my earbuds in and reclined my chair back the measly two inches it was willing to go. I was ready for the time to pass at full speed so I could be in my bed, all wrapped up in Kline. *Never Been Kissed* was the courtesy movie for my flight home, and I couldn't deny my excitement.

Even though that movie came out forever ago, it will always have one of my favorite endings. Sam Coulson running down the stadium steps.
"Don't Worry Baby" by The Beach Boys playing in the background.
The crowd cheering.
Josie Gellar watching him stride toward her.
And then, that kiss. How he just grabs her and kisses the fuck out of her.
Yeah. Talk about cinematic perfection.

I could remember watching that movie when I was young and just wishing, hoping, *fucking praying* I'd get my Josie Gellar, "Don't Worry Baby" moment. I'd truly believed that everyone got to experience one of those epically romantic moments once in their lives.

I had mine with Kline when he stood in his office—proving to me that he was every bit of the man I knew he was—and got down on one knee, asking me to spend the rest of my life with him. He'd lived up to the fantasy and then some. Sure, we'd had other amazing, swoony moments, but that one topped the rest by a landslide.

Damn, I miss my husband.

The flight had been long, and despite my valiant efforts to catch some shut-eye, I stayed wide-eyed and fidgety the whole way. After navigating my way out of baggage claim, I hopped in a cab and headed home.

I was nearly vibrating with excitement over surprising Kline.

The cab ride was short and sweet thanks to the time of morning, and with no rush-hour traffic or random construction delays to stop my progress, I was out of the cab and onto our elevator within 30 minutes.

I slipped in through the door, toeing off my heels and locking the dead bolt with a soft click. Leaving my suitcase and purse in the entry, I tiptoed down the dark hall and stopped at the doorway of our bedroom. It took a second for my eyes to adjust to the lack of light, but when they did, it didn't take long to find myself very, very confused by the number of figures lying in our bed. As I moved farther into the room, my night vision transitioned completely, and what I saw had me stopping dead in my tracks.

Kline lay on his back in his familiar sleeping pose—one leg hanging out from beneath the blankets and an arm strewn across his abdomen. And Walter was in his familiar spot, curled up at the foot of the bed.

But he wasn't alone.

Nope.

Stan was sleeping soundly on my side of the bed, his giant head resting on my pillow. And his little buddy Walter was pressed up against his stretched out legs.

Kline Brooks had officially caved on Stan.

Jesus. Could he be any swoonier?

I needed to thank him. *A lot.* Because hell, I was pretty sure he had just given me another "Don't Worry Baby" moment.

Quietly, so as not to disturb my husband, I roused Walter and Stan awake, encouraging them to slip off the bed and out of our bedroom.

Stan followed my lead with puppy-like movements, his long tail wagging and paws awkwardly tapping against the hardwood floor. Walter was less enthused, but he followed nonetheless. I had a feeling it had more to do with his boyfriend than me, but I'd take what I could get.

Guiding them into the living room, I threw an old comforter on the couch and got them settled. Within a few minutes, my two boys were sawing logs, adorably cuddled up to one another.

When I returned to the bedroom, Kline was still where I had left him, deep in sleep and looking sexy as hell with bedhead and only a pair of boxer briefs and a thin sheet covering his body.

I quickly got undressed and climbed onto the foot of the bed, crawled under the covers and stopped once I reached the waistband of his boxer briefs. When my fingers started to slide them down, Kline stirred in his sleep, his eyes blinking in confusion.

"What the…? Georgie?"

"Hi, baby," I whispered, tugging his briefs down just enough to reveal his…*oh, yeah.*

"What are you doing home so early?" he asked, rubbing at his eyes feverishly.

"I was missing you too much."

"What time is it?" His voice was thick and groggy.

"It's time for me to thank my amazing husband."

His brows lifted. "I like where this is headed, but what exactly are you thanking me for?"

I straddled his hips, leaning forward to brush my mouth against his. "You caved on Stan," I said, tugging on his bottom lip.

He grinned. "Oh, yeah, Stan."

"Oh, yeah, *him*. The giant dog that was just sleeping on my pillow."

Kline laughed as his fingers slid into my hair, tangling with the loose curls. "Walter's boyfriend snores, by the way. *A lot.*"

I giggled, but I needed to ask, "What made you change your mind?"

"Your happiness is my happiness," he said, like it was the most normal thing in the world. "So are you happy?"

I leaned back, staring down at my stupidly romantic husband. "Yes, Mr. Brooks, I am very fucking happy. I'm literally the luckiest woman on the planet, and it's all thanks to my sweet, amazing, perfect husband." I caressed his cheek with my hand. "I love you. I love you so very much."

"Fuck, I missed you, Benny." He tugged my mouth back to his, kissing me hard and deep. He kissed me until moans hijacked my lips and my hips started to move against his instinctively.

"So…about that whole thanking your husband thing?" he asked, smirking like the devil.

"Oh, yeah, about that," I answered as I slid down his body. My lips found his skin and started a slow, seductive path down his stomach. "I'm feeling all sorts of generous this morning."

"I'm loving the sound of this," he said, his voice choppy.

"This morning," I said, wrapping my hand around his cock, "my happiness will be all about *my husband's* happiness."

"That's one hell of a cycle."

The instant my tongue tasted him, he groaned.

"*Fuck*, yeah, this is definitely making me happy."

New York, Saturday, May 14th, Morning

Kline

"Go ahead, Stan," I whispered in the late morning sunlight of our bedroom. "Get closer. Come on, scoot closer. Really crowd her."

Waking up to Georgie earlier was one of the best unexpected treats I'd ever experienced. I'd missed her an awful lot—to the point that I was starting to annoy myself. Long, drawn-out conversations with Walter and Stan weren't my idea of an ideal reality. I'd needed my wife, I'd needed her surprise, and now, I couldn't wait to give her another one of her own.

I turned to look behind me and found Walter looking on from the edge of the area rug, completely unamused. "You too. Get up here!" I whisper-yelled. "I need your help." He narrowed his eyes at me, and I mirrored the gesture right back at him. "Don't you want to show her our other surprise?"

Two more licks to his paw later, he finally moved forward and jumped up on the bed.

"Thank you."

Now I'm thanking cats? Jesus.

"Get close, guys," I instructed again, and for once, they listened.

Stan's nose nudged under the curve of Georgie's neck, and Walter laid his kitty paw on her cheek on the other side. She swiped and swatted and tried to shoo it away, but my boys were relentless.

"Georgie," I whispered, trying to help her along on the trip from Sleepytown to Awakeville.

"Bratwurst," she mumbled.

"Pickles," she went on. I laughed. "Big-dicked—"

Hell yes!

"Thor."

Fuck.

"Benny, wake up."

She moaned and tried to move, but the animals wouldn't let her, and finally, her eyes popped open in frustration. "Fucking space management, you little shits are a bigger problem than I realized," she announced immediately, seeing them and not me.

"I tried to tell you."

"Shit!" she shrieked, a hand rising to her chest as a flimsy shield. "You scared me to death."

I smiled and raised my eyebrows. "Rough wake-up call, baby?"

"No," she denied. "I was just surprised is all."

"You're drowning in paws."

"Okay," she hedged. "Maybe a little, but it's no big deal."

She was afraid I was going to take the dog back. Stan barked like he could sense it.

"I don't know." I pushed on, desperate to get her good and riled up. "I was afraid this would happen. There's no room for me in that bed, and I don't like the sound of that."

"Kline—"

"No, Benny. If there's a bed with you, I want to be in it."

"We'll get a bigger bed," she offered quickly.

"This bedroom really isn't big enough for a king."

I was expecting her to get angry, but she just looked crestfallen. *Shit.*

Tears threatened the corners of her pretty blue eyes, and I knew I'd do anything to stop them. Striding to the bed, I shoved Walter out of the way with a hiss and cupped her cheek.

"Don't cry, baby. I was just messing with you. Stan's here to stay, I swear."

Her waterfall of melancholy dried up faster than a raindrop.

"What the fuck? Were you faking those tears?"

"Maybe," she admitted with a smirk.

Fuck. I would have fucking sworn those tears were real. "I don't like this. I don't like this one bit."

"I'm sorry," she laughed. "I promise to never trap you with fake tears if you promise to always keep Stan."

I had no plans to get rid of Stan. Quite frankly, I kind of liked him. "Deal."

She smiled again and wrapped her arms around my neck, and it took a full thirty seconds before I realized my perfectly crafted plan hadn't been executed even close to the blueprints.

"Shit."

"What?" she asked, pulling back to look at me.

"Nothing. Just…that didn't go according to plan at all. I started that whole mess for a reason."

"A reason?"

"A big one," I clarified with a playful wince.

"Just spit it out!" she yelled through a laugh, smacking me on the chest.

So I did.

"You want to go see our new house?"

"House? As in…a house?!"

"It's the housiest house *I've* ever seen," I joked.

"Oh, my God! I fucking love housey houses!" she shouted and stage dived directly off the bed and even deeper into my heart.

She was perfect in all of her awkward excitement, and I was just the man at her mercy.

"I love you," I told her, just as her mouth met mine.

"Me too," she said. "I can't believe you did this. Why? Why did you do this?"

"Because you want the dog, and Walter wants the dog, and that means I want Stan too. Stan means fucking space. This'll give it to us."

"*Kline.*"

"We'll always miss you when you're gone, but when you come back, you'll always know we're all happy and healthy and waiting completely impatiently at home."

New York, Tuesday, May 16ᵗʰ, Very Early Morning

Thatch

Kline and Georgia had been back from their honeymoon for two weeks, and already, the fucker had gone and gotten her a house *and* a dog. He was sick in the head, but if you asked me, that was the definition of love. I hated that they were moving out of the city, but they still worked here, and Kline never went out anyway. I'd just have to travel a little farther when I felt like crashing on their couch. Otherwise, my life would remain pretty much the same.

My phone chirping over the hum of needles pulled my attention away from my friend Frankie's latest portrait tattoo. Some guy from Detroit had driven all the way here just for Frankie's unique talent. I still got a kick out of that shit.

When I picked up my phone, a text message from a number I didn't recognize read like a fucking novel.

> **Unknown: The Mingan Island Cetacean Study Group has been using photographic techniques to study humpback whales for the last 16 years. In that time, they began to realize that female humpback whales not only make friends with one another, but they reunite each year.**
> **Isn't that adorable! Such cuties!**
> **If you've received this message in error, please text Unsubscribe. If you're ready for another complementary fact, text Whale Lover.**

What in the ever-loving fuck is this shit?

> *Me: UNSUBSCRIBE*

> **Unknown: If you would like to unsubscribe from Interesting Whale Facts of the Day, text yes. But we really hope you don't because we'd sure miss you!**

> *Me: YES.*

Unknown: YES, PLEASE! You just received a superspecial subscription to Sexy Words of the Day. There's nothing sexier than a man whispering, "You're beautiful," into a woman's ear.

What the fucking fuck? My fingers tapped violently across the screen.

Me: Goddammit. I don't want this.

Unknown: We had an issue with processing your request. If you'd like to unsubscribe from Sexy Words of the Day, text yes.

Me: FUCK YES. UNSUBSCRIBE YOU STUPID MOTHERFUCKERS.

Unknown: You're a dirty, dirty boy who just received a free picture subscription to Spank Me Daddy. Are you ready for your first picture? Text yes, if you are.

Okay. I'd been frustrated, but fuck if I wasn't intrigued by this turn of events.

Me: YES

Unknown: Uh-oh, you just unsubscribed from Spank Me Daddy. We're going to be so sad you're leaving.

Me: I said YES, cocksucker. Fucking hell, you need better IT.

Unknown: Did someone just say the secret password?

Oh, yeah! Now we were speaking the same language.

Me: Cocksucker? That's my secret password?

Unknown: Yes, he did! You've just won 30 days of getting to watch Cassie masturbate without getting to touch her. Congratulations, dickwad.

Unknown: Oh, hey, by the way, I got a new number.

Goddammit, this fucking girl. She was pure evil. I hadn't heard from her since we'd parted ways in front of the coffee shop. I glanced around the crowded tattoo parlor and found no one was paying me or my half chub any attention. It was nearing one a.m., but this was when the place got really busy. Everyone was occupied.

I assigned her name to this number and shot her a reply.

*Me: *whispering into your ear* You're beautiful, Cassie.*

Cass: I know. You should see me right now. Bent forward at the waist. Legs spread. And...

Jesus Christ.

Me: And what? What are you doing, babe?

Cass: Touching...Lots of touching...

Yes. Hell yes.

Cass: Phones. Touching phones, you perv. Verizon has a strict pants policy.

Verizon? What the hell? I glanced around one more time before stepping out onto the sidewalk and pushing the little phone at the top of her message.

She answered on the first ring.

"Well, hello, Thatcher. You sure are a naughty boy, Daddy."

I chuckled. "I'm only as naughty as you want me to be, honey."

"How are you? Out chasing pussy?" she asked, and my eyebrows pinched together. She sounded like she was fishing.

I looked back inside the shop through the glass door and back down to the sidewalk. "No. At work, actually."

"Work?" she yelled. "It's like middle-of-the-night o'clock there too, isn't it?"

"Ah, but I'm a man of many mysteries. You didn't think I just had the one job, did you?"

"Well, yeah. I fucking did."

I laughed. "I told you. I have my hands in *everything*."

"I just figured that was a euphemism for pussy."

Frankie's gaze jerked toward me through the door at the sound of my booming laughter, and I shook my head at him. "What are you doing with a new number? If you lost your phone, you can just get a new one, you know."

"Fuck that shit. And I didn't lose my phone. I'm fucking responsible."

"Right," I lied.

"I am. That's what the number change is all about, actually. The last four digits spell out 'Cass' now. How fucking great is that?"

My eyebrows pinched together again. "You changed your number so that you'd have a text acronym at the end?"

"Yes! I had a late afternoon shoot, and then went for a couple of drinks with the guys afterward."

"The guys?"

"And we were talking and drinking, and it just hit me. I had to change my number."

I was curious about the guys. Really fucking curious. But now I was curious about other things. "You're drunk right now?"

"Tipsy," she admitted.

Jesus. All that whale shit and subterfuge. "You're probably the most proficient drunk texter I've ever encountered in my life," I said and laughed.

"Baby," drunk Cassie cooed, and my dick swelled from half cocked to fully loaded. "I'm proficient at *all kinds of things.*"

Bahamas, Tuesday, May 16^(th), Very Early Morning

Cassie

"I'm all ears, honey." His husky voice vibrated against my cheek.

I ran my finger across the rim of my margarita glass and then slid it into my mouth, sucking the salt off. The jury was still out on why Thatch had been my first text from my new number, but for some odd reason, he was.

I couldn't help myself. I just really liked screwing with him—he took any shit I gave with ease and tossed it right back. And if I was being honest, I really fucking liked it. Not many men could handle my version of sarcasm. But, Thatch? Yeah, he handled it all right, seemingly entertained by whatever came out of my mouth.

Well, that and my tits. Yeah, he found them entertaining too.

"Put your boner away, Thatcher," I teased him with our running joke. An inside fucking joke. With Thatcher Kelly. *What was the world coming to?*

"You started this," he said, and I could picture his sexy smirk. "What are your tits wearing, Cass?"

"None of your business." I laughed. And smiled.

"Oh, but it is my business. Your tits and I are on a first-name basis. We're like Pam and Jim. P, B, and motherfucking J."

I kept smiling. "You watch *The Office*?"

"Would Kline eat dog shit for Georgia? Of course, I watch *The Office*."

"I take it you heard about Stan."

"Yeah," he said with a chuckle. "I owe Kline a lot of favors thanks to you losing their cat."

"I did not lose their cat!" I exclaimed, and nearly everyone in the bar turned in my direction. "Oh, fuck off! This is a bar, not a goddamn library!" I shouted toward no asshole in particular.

"Starting your UFC career in the Bahamas doesn't sound like a good idea, Cass," Thatch said. "I thought you agreed to be good?" His voice was edged with something my drunken brain couldn't decipher.

"Yeah, but it's your version of good. That leaves room for a lot of possibilities."

He ignored the jab. "Promise me something, honey."

"And what would that be?"

"No Fight Club unless I'm with you."

"Ohhh…Thatcher doesn't think I'm strong enough to take care of myself?" I retorted sarcastically.

"I *know* you are, Cass," he responded immediately.

"Then why would I need you around?"

"Because I *want* to be there. I don't want anything to happen to you."

My chest felt tingly and weird. "Well…that's really kind of sweet of you to say."

"I can be sweet, honey. I can be real fucking sweet when I want to be."

"Cass! We're getting ready to head out. You comin'?" Arnoldo yelled from the bar as he closed out his tab.

"Who was that?" Thatch asked.

"Arnoldo," I answered. "He's one of the models I've been work-ing with down here."

The phone went silent for a few beats, and for some odd reason, I felt the need to add a few more details. "Arnoldo is crazy good-look-ing…and getting over a harsh breakup with his boyfriend. I told him we could spend the rest of the night in my hotel room, stuffing our faces with room service and trashing stupid men."

He chuckled. "Sounds like a party."

"You know it." I got up from my barstool and grabbed my purse. "I better go. I've got a guy to console, feed, and shove off to bed, before I rub one out and call it a night."

"Tell your tits I miss them."

"I'll be sure to pass along the message."

"Do that while you're spread-eagled on your bed and getting yourself off to thoughts of me."

"I would, but you haven't given me anything to have thoughts about."

Yeah, yeah, I know that was a lie.
Of course, he'd given me things to think about. I had felt his cock.
Believe me, I had a lot of fucking thoughts about that monster.

"I accept that challenge."

God, he was like the king of one-upping.

"Good night, Cass. Be good."

"Be sweet, Thatch," I said and then ended the call.

Be sweet? Did I really just say that?

Hell, Thatcher Kelly hadn't crawled inside my brain and start-ed demanding attention. And I knew, without a doubt, this situa-tion had nowhere else to go but down…and up…and back down again…on the Jolly Green Giant's cock.

THE END

Love Kline, Georgia, and the crew?

Stay up to date with them and us by signing up for our newsletter: www.authormaxmonroe.com/#!contact/c1kcz

You may live to regret much, but we promise it won't be this.

Seriously. We'll make it fun.

If you're already signed up, consider sending us a message to tell us how much you love us. We really like that. ;)

And you really don't want to miss Cassie making good on her promise, right?

#IdThatchThat

Cassie and Thatch are coming for you next in *Banking the Billionaire* (Billionaire Bad Boys Book 2) on July 26, 2016.

CONTACT INFORMATION

Follow us online:

Website: www.authormaxmonroe.com

Facebook: www.facebook.com/authormaxmonroe

Reader Group:www.facebook.com/groups/1561640154166388

Twitter: www.twitter.com/authormaxmonroe

Instagram: www.instagram.com/authormaxmonroe

Goodreads: https://goo.gl/8VUIz2

ACKNOWLEDGEMENTS

First of all, THANK YOU for reading. That goes for anyone who's bought a copy, read an ARC, helped us beta, edited, or found time in their busy schedule just to make sure we didn't completely fuck over Kline and Georgie…or Walter. We know some of you are here for that asshole.

Thank you for supporting us, for talking about our books, and for just being so unbelievably loving and supportive of our characters. You've made this our MOST favorite adventure thus far.

THANK YOU to each other. Monroe is thanking Max. Max is thanking Monroe. This shouldn't surprise you since we did this in the first book. Or maybe it does surprise you because you didn't read those acknowledgements. Fuck you very much, Leslie. Well, in case you missed it, we'll say it again. And again. We'll actually probably do this forever.

We've found something special together, and to be honest, it doesn't even have that much to do with books. Doing this together has helped us through some pretty awful times, made every day exciting, and turned it into something that we want to keep on doing, for as long as we can keep on doing it.

THANK YOU, Lisa, for being your amazing, hilarious, and eagle-eyed self. We couldn't have finished this book without you. Well, we finished it, but we would have had to publish the pig slop that is any first draft. And really, we couldn't have published the first book without you, and if that was the case, Tapping Her would still be a figment of our imaginations. Good thing you're so awesome and flexible. ;)

THANK YOU, Kristin, for helping us put out as clean a product as possible. Your spit really makes us shine. (Disclaimer: When we say spit, we mean Kristin's talented proofing eyes. Don't worry, she's never spit on us or at us or anywhere near us. No spitting. Just perfect proofing.)

THANK YOU, Murphy, for being superhuman and multi-tasking while growing, birthing, and raising a super-adorable-human. You're the best.

THANK YOU, Amy, for pretending to laugh at our jokes even when they probably aren't funny. We're just starting out on this journey with you, but we've got all kinds of feelings telling us it's going to be incredible. That could be indigestion from the donuts, but we're going with "feelings."

THANK YOU, JoAnna & Sandra, for being superior Counselor Feathers. You ladies amaze us on a daily basis, and you are the reason Camp Love Yourself is the coolest place to be. Seriously, you do a better job of running it than we do.

THANK YOU, Sommer, for recreating the perfect piece of Honeymoon Heaven in a cover. When we look at it, we can *feel* our characters. They've only touched us inappropriately once or twice.

THANK YOU to every blogger who has read, reviewed, posted, shared, and supported us. Your enthusiasm, support, and hard work does not go unnoticed. We wish we could send you your very own Kline as thanks. We can't. And even if we could, we don't think he'd go willingly, and we're not really comfortable walking that fine a line with human trafficking.

THANK YOU, to our families. They support us, motivate us, and most importantly, tolerate us. Sometimes we're not the easiest people to live with, especially when there is a deadline looming. We honestly don't know what we'd do without you guys.

Hey. Cool it with the ego, cocksuckers. You guys can be assholes too. It's not just us.

THANK YOU, to our favorite ladies in the infamous Camp Love Yourself Bora Bora Thread. You know who you are. You are crazy, hilarious, and so fucking cool. #YouveThatchedThat #CLYScoutsHonor

And last but not least, THANK YOU, to everyone who participated in our Tapping You giveaway. We loved reading your awkward and awesome stories, and we'll be laughing about some of them for probably the rest of time. But don't worry, we're totally laughing *with* you.

As always, all our love.

TAPPING YOU

Thank you so much to everyone who submitted a story, voted, shared, commented, liked, and bought this book. We hope you loved our little addition to Kline and Georgia and have your seatbelt on in preparation for Cassie and Thatch in *Banking the Billionaire*.

But our characters needed some help for this bonus material, so we enlisted you guys and your real life love stories.

These stories based on the entries by Christin and Melissa bear little to no resemblance to the original stories, so don't blame them for what you're about to read.

We hope you'll all be forever lucky in love.

XO,
Max Monroe

"AN UNPRE(DICK)TABLE EVENING"

Thatch

"You've been to this place before?" I asked Cassie as we stepped inside Zero Dark Flirty. This was one of the most random choices of bars in Manhattan I'd ever been forced into entertaining, but I didn't ask probing or detailed questions. Those kinds of questions led to answers, and answers usually led to some form of physical pain. Suddenly fearful of a surprise attack, I realized I could barely see Cassie through the darkness and was hoping my eyes would adjust quickly.

"Oh yeah, totally."

"You're lying, aren't you?"

"Oh yeah, totally," she repeated through a laugh.

I smiled and shook my head. "Just wait until Georgia and Kline get here. You'll never hear the end of it if he can't see his menu."

"Fuck Big-dick and his old man eyes, Thatcher."

I bit my lip to stop myself from telling her how dark it really was in here. I wasn't big on many things, but I was big on sexual restitution for whatever suffering I'd experienced during the day, and trust me, the way to get it from Cassie was not by complaining.

"Hey!" she shouted and pointed toward an even darker corner of the bar. "That's my friend Christin!"

How the fuck she could tell, I had no clue. All I could see were the vague shadows of a couple canoodling. Or fucking. Or fighting. Really, they could have been doing absolutely anything.

I'd have to take her at her word. "Should we go say hi?"

"Yeah. She's had a really bad string of luck with men, so we'll bail her out if we need to."

As we got closer, so did Christin and her date, and I had a feeling we wouldn't be needing to bail Christin out of anything.

"Christin! Hey!" Cassie greeted as we stopped in front of their table. Christin's head whipped toward us and the whites of her eyes brightened the dark room just slightly.

"Oh my God! Cassie Phillips! I haven't seen you in forever!"

"I know!"

They hugged and gabbed like girls tend to do until Christin's eyes finally found my chest, and then moved up and up until they locked on my face.

"Holy hell. Who is this monster of a man?"

I reached out a hand with a smile as she tossed her blond hair over her shoulder. "I'm Thatch."

"Christin."

"Nice to meet you."

"You too!" She turned to the table and reached for her date, glancing back to me in the process. "This is my date—oh shit!"

Her martini glass bounced and shattered and the cool liquid spilled everywhere in a rush, coating her date's stomach and pants and making him jump from his seat.

"Shite!" he shouted in a deep Scottish brogue, and we all lunged toward the table to help him.

He laughed, though, and immediately, I was relieved to know I wasn't going to have to assault some fucking random dude I'd just met for getting out of line over an honest accident.

"I guess it's a good thing I don't have a dick, yeah?"

We all started to laugh, and then I could have sworn I heard the mental screech.

"Wait…what?" I asked at the same time Cassie managed a, "Huh?"

Christin's response was rightfully more dramatic. "What the *fuck*?"

"What?" he asked, and I shuddered at the flames in Christin's eyes.

"Oh shit," Cassie muttered, and I agreed with a nod. It was about to go down.

"It seems we've had a communication breakdown," I attempted to mediate.

"Fuck yeah, we have," Christin shouted, and it started to become clear why she and Cassie were friends.

I pulled her back and settled her next to Cassie when her body made threats of physical violence. "I think what Christin's trying to say—"

"I need the D to get down!"

"Is that she had a fantastic time with you—"

"My pussy needs a pirate!"

"But it's not really gonna work out."

I winced, but pulled the women away before things got even more awkward.

We bellied up the bar and Cassie tried to comfort a distraught Christin. This wasn't exactly how she'd planned the evening.

"This is why you always do a dick grab early on," Cassie advised sagely, and I shook my head with a laugh.

"Like, how early on?" Christin asked.

"Do not listen to Cassie," I cut in.

"Excuse me!" Cassie yelled. "She'll fucking listen to me." She turned to Christin and smiled. "Thatcher isn't a woman—"

"I'll say," Christin interjected.

"So he's never been in this situation."

I laughed. "Have *you* been in this situation? I think not."

Cassie's eyes narrowed dramatically, and I put a hand over my crotch protectively. She smirked and replied, "No. Not exactly. But I have a vagina and I can empathize."

I moved my hand when it looked like Cassie's aggression had cooled and offered up a question. "So what would you do? To make her feel better now?" I looked to Christin and raised my eyebrows. "You want to feel better now, right?"

I thought she would answer, but her eyes left mine and didn't return. I couldn't tell what she was looking at until it happened. One minute I was standing there innocently, and the next I was being fondled.

"What the fuck?" I shouted with a laugh as Christin's hand closed around my cock and gave it a squeeze. She didn't answer, but instead closed her eyes and breathed deep for a full two seconds.

My panicked eyes shot to Cassie, but she just laughed.

"There," Christin said as she released my confused cock. "I feel better now."

Kline and Georgia arrived right then.

"Hey, guys!" Georgia waved sweetly while Kline stepped up beside her.

Still in shock, I did the only thing I could. Introduced my fondler. "This is Christin."

Kline smiled and stuck out his hand, but the dick grabbing fiend wasn't done. Right past his hand she reached straight to his pants and grabbed his Big-dicked Brooks without shame.

"Oh, holy shit!" Kline shrieked, his voice taking on a pitch way higher than his normal.

"What the fuck?" Georgia yelled, just as Cassie pulled a smiling

Christin back.

"I'm sorry," she said, her voice completely unapologetic. "But you just completely saved my night."

Cassie laughed and then verbalized, "Yeah," as she wrapped her arm around Christin's shoulders and turned her away from the bar. "I'd say it's time for a girls' pow-wow. C'mon, Georgia."

Georgia glanced at Kline, then at me, and then shrugged, before following the girls toward the bathroom.

Cassie

"Feel better?" I asked Christin once we were inside the bathroom.

She nodded as her lips crested into an amused grin.

"Well, I don't feel better," Georgia interjected with an irritated scowl. "I gotta say, Christin, I'm not too thrilled about your grabby hands touching my husband's dick."

"Yeah, that wasn't cool, Christin," I partially agreed, "but I get it."

"Wait. What do you mean you get it?" Georgia asked in outrage.

"Well, Christin here was on a date with someone she thought was a handsome Scottish dude. But her date ended up being a chick, no dick."

"What?" Georgia exclaimed and her eyes damn near bugged out of her head.

"Yeah," Chrisin chimed in. "Talk about a shitty fucking night."

"Jesus, that's awful," Georgia said and her irritation dissipated in a matter of seconds as she pulled Christin in for a tight hug. "I take back what I said. If you need to grab Kline's dick again, please feel free."

Mother Brooks', ladies and gentleman, the patron saint of dicks.

"Honestly, I think the two dick grabs really helped me find my happy place," Christin said with a giggle. "My faith in humanity is restored, and both dicks gave me hope that the right man is out there for me—and packing a pipe."

"No one tell Thatch you had that kind of revelation from touching his cock. He'll think it needs a fucking cape and a tattooed 'S' on his shaft."

Both Christin and Georgia laughed.

"What do you want to do tonight, honey?" I asked. "No way we're letting you go home to eat Ben & Jerry's and watch porn."

"Yeah, that's strictly for Tuesdays," Georgia teased.

"I want to drink all of the alcohol in New York," Christin announced as she freshened up her lip gloss.

"What do you think, Wheorgie? Should we leave the men for the night?"

Georgia nodded. "Yeah, let's fucking do it. No way we're letting our girl drink by herself."

Fifteen minutes and two promises of blow jobs later, Georgia, Christin, and I were headed to Barcelona Bar. The second we arrived, I ordered three Harry Potter shots and convinced the house band to play *Boys* by Britney Spears. We downed the shots and hopped on stage, dancing and singing our asses off.

Homegirl was a bit of a freak on the floor, dropping it real low and bringing it back with a hypnotic shake of her hips. She was getting looks from all sides of the room, but the drummer behind her seemed to be showing the most interest. He was hot by all accounts—defined arms, chiseled jawline and a pair of sexy-as-hell green eyes that would've had me licking my lips and fluffing my boobs back in the day.

Yeah, he was *all* man, and it was safe to say, Christin's night was about to take a huge change for the better.

I glanced at Georgia and nodded toward the drummer's eyes. Eyes that were locked on our friend's *ass*-ets.

Georgia grinned and danced with Christin while simultaneously leading her closer and closer to the drummer. The second the backs of her thighs hit the side of the drummer's legs, Georgia went in for the kill, bumping Christin with her hips and forcing her to fall into his lap. He barely missed a beat, adjusting her between his thighs and drumming around her body.

She glanced up into his hypnotizing green eyes and he smirked, offering a sexy wink in her direction.

Christin stayed like that—perched right between the drummer's thighs—while Georgia and I were content to watch from the bar. Between sets he'd whisper into her ear and she'd reciprocate with a flirty giggle and grin. By the last few songs of the night, his strong hands were wrapped around hers as he taught her how to bang it out on the drums.

I had a feeling that wasn't going to be the only banging before the night was through.

And that feeling was made truth when they announced last call and Christin met us at the bar as we gathered our purses and called a cab.

"So, I'm going to go home with Channing," she whispered.

"Excuse me?" I asked. "That drummer's name is Channing?"

Christin nodded and a wicked smile curved her pretty lips upward.

Georgia burst into laughter.

"You've got to be fucking kidding me," I muttered.

Christin's expression changed to confused.

"You'll have to excuse Cassie, but she has a thing for names, and well, Channing is like her name if you know what I'm sayin'."

Christin giggled. "It's a hot name."

"Yeah," I agreed. "You get to go bang the hot drummer named

Channing and I have to head home to deal with the Jolly Green Giant."

"Who also happens to be named Thatch and has a dick the size of my forearm," Christin added.

I thought it over for a few seconds.

"Yeah, you're right. I'll just re-name his dick Channing and I'll be set for the night."

Georgia gestured for the door. "Come on, crazy. Our cab's here."

As we hugged Christin goodbye, Channing stepped up to our group and wrapped his hand around her waist. "You ladies our bloody fantastic dancers," he said in a sexy British accent.

"Oh for the love of porn GIFs!" I shouted and held both hands out in the air. "Drummer? Channing? British?"

A confused yet amused grin spread across his full lips.

Georgia laughed and pushed me toward the door before I could say anything else. "Have fun tonight!" she called over her shoulder.

I glanced back to find Channing leaning against the bar with his arms locked around Christin, while his lips gave her one insanely hot kiss.

Yeah, our work here was done.

Christin and Channing.

Lucky bitch.

"PLAYFUL PRINCE"

Kline

Cynthia's eyes met mine across the common area as John sang to Melissa, and they weren't the least bit amused.

"Baby, who wants to love me sexy, uh?" John sang from his knees, grabbing at Melissa's hips and forcing her to dance along to the imaginary music.

I wanted to smile because John might have been clown, but it still took a certain amount of both balls and interest to shamelessly serenade a woman in front of a crowd. You had to be willing to subject yourself to whatever humiliation came your way at whatever price it came.

But I could see the wheels spinning in Cynthia's mind with every word John sang. And her thoughts weren't focused on the lyrics. Instead, they were fueled by Human Resource's policies and procedures regarding conduct in the workplace.

"Baby, are you ready to lick me sexy uh uh."

This is all your fault, Kline Brooks, I could practically hear her brain shouting at me.

"Take off your shoes and suck me sexy."

This is the kind of thing that's going to get us sued, Kline Brooks.

"Baby, we're naked and we're humpin' sexy."

Yikes. She's probably going to blow her lid if I don't stop this soon.

Melissa smiled and giggled the smile of a woman who was trying not to be amused. Honestly, it reminded me of Georgia when she tried to convince me she was mad at me.

No doubt in my mind, Melissa was head over heels and by the increased enthusiasm on John's part, I wasn't the only who noticed.

I had to give it to John, he'd been pursuing her relentlessly for months, trying to get her to cave with sweet notes and surprise lunches in the office fridge. He always went the extra mile, and while I appreciated it, Cynthia didn't like what it meant for the office.

The crowd of employees clapped as Melissa got down on her knees and agreed to all sorts of things, but Cynthia's eyes never released mine. They had the intensity of a hawk as she summoned me into her office with a flick of her fingers.

I crossed the space and entered the room with ease, taking a seat in the chair across from her desk and trying to wipe the smile off my face. I felt like I'd been called to the principal's office to be reprimanded at my *own* school.

"Mr. Brooks—" she started, and I immediately cut in. Her voice was tense enough for the both of us.

"Relax, Cynthia. Everyone seemed to enjoy it."

"Right. Everyone seemed to enjoy it. Until you find out about meek little Britney, the new intern who just experienced a date rape at college and now fears for her safety from pursuit at work."

"Jesus. That's terrible. When did we hire her? Is she okay? Do you think we need to set up some kind of—"

"There's no Britney."

"What?"

"I made her up," she clarified.

"Fuck, Cynthia. You just made that shit up? That's awful. Why on earth is that the scenario living in your mind?"

"Because it could happen."

"I hope not." Jesus. I had chest pain just thinking about imaginary Britney and her awful ordeal.

"We need to put a no fraternization policy in the new hire contract."

"Cyn—"

"*This* is why. That was innocent to you, but it's not innocent to everyone."

"I appreciate where you're coming from and this is a prime example of why I will forever entrust you as Director of Human Resources."

"But?" she questioned with a hand going straight to her hip.

I scrubbed a hand down my face in frustration. "Just give me a minute to think this through before you go guns blazing and drop kick John's lovesick ass out the door."

"Fine. But, you can expect twenty-four hours of silence on my end and then, I won't stop bothering you for a resolution."

Jesus, this woman almost had as much bite as my Georgie when she was fired up.

I left the office that day feeling sick over the entire situation. Neither John nor Melissa deserved any bullshit reprimands for being attracted to one another.

Hell, if anything, John deserved an award for his persistence and Melissa deserved a million dollars for staying strong as long as she did.

I called Georgia on my way home that night, giving her the down and dirty on John's explicit lyrics and Cynthia's overall irritation. She had been in San Diego for the past week while the Mavericks played the Chargers and I was more than ready for her to be home.

"Man, she's a bit of a hardass," Georgia responded. "Honestly, I'm surprised she didn't sue you for going through her files to find out I was Rose."

"Truer words have never been spoken, Benny."

"What are you going to do?"

I stared out the window as Frank maneuvered through traffic. "I miss you. And I was kind of hoping my beautiful, brilliant wife would have the answer to that question."

"Aw, I miss you too, baby. But don't worry, I'll be heading home in less than twenty-four hours."

"Thank fuck for that."

She giggled. "But seriously, what are you going to do? Cynthia won't let this one go."

"What do you think I should do?"

"Well…I actually think the whole thing is pretty goddamn adorable. It makes me miss working with everyone. God, I bet Dean was beside himself when John was serenading Melissa."

"Pretty sure I saw him recording it. And baby?"

"Yeah?" she asked, voice soft.

"There's always a job offer waiting for you. You say the word and I'll send over the contract."

She laughed. "Pretty sure that's offer number three for the day, Brooks."

"There's a reason they say third time's the charm."

"Not this time. And you should probably think about limiting yourself to one offer a day," she pointed out.

"What can I say? I'm persistent and highly motivated by the idea of mid-afternoon sex in my office with my insanely hot wife on a daily basis."

"I've got two ideas for you. You ready to hear them?"

"If one of them includes you naked, yes."

"Monday afternoon, I'll stop by your office and show you some of my very best moves."

"Fuck, *yes*. And please, for the love of God, wear my favorite black stilettos."

"Deal," she agreed on a giggle. "Okay and now to idea number two. Let John go. Give him one hell of a severance package and tell him to apply for the new position that just opened with the Mavericks. Tell him it comes with great benefits, more than he's currently getting paid, and tickets to any NFL game he wants to see."

"How big of a severance package?"

"If I were in Melissa's shoes, I'd hope it would big enough for a big fat engagement ring, my dream wedding, and one hell of a honeymoon."

"What in the fuck kind of shoes does Melissa wear? *Louboutins?*"

She laughed. "I'm telling Dean you said that."

I sighed. "You really think that's the best option?"

"I think it's the nicest option. John is a hard worker, but Melissa has been with Brooks Media longer. Plus, what twenty-something guy wouldn't want to work for an NFL team?"

"Damn you drive you an expensive bargain, woman."

"You should talk to my husband," she said with amusement in her voice. "It took him offering to sign over his entire company to convince me to marry him."

I chuckled fondly at her twist on the sequence of events. "Your husband sounds like a genius."

"Yeah," she agreed. "His brain is almost as big as his cock."

"Keep talking like that and I'll be on the first flight out to San Diego," I growled into the phone.

"How about a video chat tonight once I'm all tucked into my hotel suite?"

"Consider me hard and ready, baby."

Three months later, Georgia and I were seated in attendance at John and Melissa's lavish wedding inside The Plaza Hotel in New York. Candles lit the room with a warm ambience, lush flowers filled the space with an exquisite aroma, and the bride was blushing and beautiful in her wedding gown and veil.

John stood proudly at the altar, listening to Melissa recite her hand-written vows, and his eyes were over-flowing with the kind of sentiment only a groom desperately in love with his bride could portray.

"And each day, you would do things that would make me fall more and more, until I not only realized I was in love in with you, but that I wanted to spend the rest of my life with you. I love you, John. I will always love you, no matter what obstacles may come our way because you're my best friend."

The groom smiled down at his bride as he cupped her cheeks and swiped a few tears from beneath her eyes, mouthing, "I love you."

When the minister said, "You may kiss the bride," John didn't hold back, shouting, "Fuck yes!" as he wrapped Melissa up in his arms and kissed the hell out of her.

Everyone in attendance cheered, clapped, and laughed as Melissa and John walked down the aisle, hand-in-hand, and their newlywed eyes filled with nothing but love for one another.

And do you want to know the ironically funny thing about the sequence of events that led to John and Melissa's three-month courtship turned marriage?

Remember that severance package Georgia told me to offer John?

When he asked me what he should tell everyone at Brooks Media about his abrupt exit, I responded with, "Hell, I don't care. Tell them you won the lottery."

As a joke, I tossed in a few lottery tickets to make him laugh, but the joke was on me.

That lucky bastard hit the motherfucking jackpot.

Not only did John's severance package from Brooks Media make him thirty million dollars richer, but it allowed the happy couple to quit their jobs and spend their days traveling the world.

Rome. Paris. Amsterdam. Hawaii. Costa Rica. Greece. Sri Lanka.

Those were just a few of the destinations they'd managed in the past three months. And after they enjoyed their reception, they would be on the first flight to Belize to start the first half of the four-month long honeymoon.

Georgie and I couldn't have been happier for them.

Mazel tov!

Thanks for reading! Don't forget to see what else we have in store for you at authormaxmonroe.com
The sky's the limit, and we won't stop until we get there.

Made in United States
Orlando, FL
12 March 2022

15712077R00085